To Amber and Amelia,

CW00865336

Atalia and the Secrets at San Gimignano

L. G. MorGan

My thanks to everyone who has encouraged and supported me in the writing of this book, particularly my family, and my friend Trish, who has spent hours reading and re-reading this text as it has been written. I am most grateful for all your help and questions as well as your insistence on getting this work complete.

Chapter 1

'It's not fair,' said Jaq, slumping himself down in front of the continental breakfast his mother had just laid out on the table for him. 'Why do I have to go to school and she doesn't?'

'We've had this discussion before, Jaq. Atalia doesn't need to go to school.'

'But she's only eleven!' Jaq stabbed the butter with his knife in frustration before spreading it aggressively across the toast. 'I wish I didn't have to go to school.'

'Look,' replied his mother, throwing down the cloth that she was using to dry last night's plates. 'You need to have a good education. If you want a good future here in Italy, you need to work hard. Focus on your own goals and dreams and don't get wound up about…'

She paused as Atalia walked into the room. 'Morning.'

Jaq grunted a similar reply, before picking up the remainder of his breakfast and walking over to the sink with his plate.

'Aren't you going to change before you go to school?' enquired his mother.

Jaq shook his head. 'No. I am wearing this.' He was stood in a pair of old yellow cropped shorts, his khaki green t-shirt that still had the paint stains on it from last summer, a pair of flip-flops and his black Juventus cap which was naturally put on back to front. Forget protecting his eyes from the sun – it was style!

'But you look scruffy…' replied Atalia, sitting down at the table, wearing her blue summer dress, a favourite of hers, that she had been given when she first joined the Alfonsi family a year or so ago. *Amazingly it still fits her*, thought Jaq, surprised that Atalia hadn't somehow grown bigger for her age.

'I am wearing this because it's Tuesday!' retorted Jaq. His mother raised an eyebrow suspiciously. 'Tuesday's are the messiest day at school and I hate Tuesdays. My clothes are simply reflecting the mood.' With that, he swallowed down the last mouthful of orange juice and went upstairs to finish getting ready.

Twenty minutes later he was in the kitchen again grabbing a croissant and a slice of watermelon to take to school for the mid-morning break. He would be home again in time for lunch before the afternoon siesta.

Mrs. Alfonsi watched him from the window as Jaq threw his bag on his back and head off to the local secondary school just outside the little town of San Gimignano.

The best thing about the school was the old sports court that stood behind the old school buildings. It was overshadowed by the fourteen old towers that stood high on the hillside – a touristic landmark that had visitors from across the country and continent flocking in by the coach loads every summer. This was seconded by the fact that the village also sold the World's Best Ice-Cream. Well, two of the ice-cream parlours in the village did, which in Jaq's mind seemed a slight contradiction in terms.

Marco was waiting for him just inside the school gates, holding his legendary basketball in his hand. He had apparently received the ball during a visit to the USA last year and had it signed by the renowned player, Gio Marvins. Jaq hadn't heard of him, neither had anyone else at school, but as Marco was a good friend and an excellent basketball player, he didn't want to upset him.

'What's up, Jaq?'

'You know what's up. It's Tuesday. Everyone hates Tuesday. It's double Italian, double Maths, double Philosophy and double ESL.'

'Oh yeah – English for Sore Losers'.

'No, Marco. English as a Secondary Language.'

'I knew that…'

A loud, piercing bell rang out from the little steeple on the top of the old school hall and everyone started shunting off from the playground in different directions.

*

The philosophy classroom was looking bare. All the posters had been removed. The teacher's desk at the front had nothing but two pens, one black, one orange, on it. The benches and tables sat redundant, looking sad and neglected following years of use; the covering of black pen writing – one table that had been inscribed with the words 'I think because I think I should.'

Jaq and Marco normally turned up late for this lesson quite deliberately. It was a tradition in which the boys would seem quite what terrible philosophical argument they could construct as their excuse. Today however, it didn't work. There was no teacher in the classroom. The rest of the class laughed at the fact that for once they had been caught out.

Minutes later however the door opened and in walked a teacher they had never seen before. His presence demanded attention. He walked with deliberate steps. His countenance was serious and determined. His cream trousers, navy blue short sleeved shirt and the jacket over his shoulder were pristine. He unpacked his bag on the desk, revealing a pile of books that appeared to have lived through a few decades of teaching to date. This was a stark contrast to the scatty Mrs. Manini that they had grown to love and adore for her shockingly untidy black hair and her chaotic organisational skills that meant lessons were rarely productive whilst she scrambled through papers and books to find the very lesson that she was looking for. This new teacher was going to be different.

Jaq and Marco looked at each other. Was this man a temp? They watched as he turned to the blackboard, picked up a piece of chalk and wrote 'Mr. Dino'.

'You can call me Sir,' he said abruptly. He started writing on the chalkboard.

Dino looked around the room. His eyes fell directly onto Marco. 'What do you understand by this phrase, boy?'

Marco's face went red as he fumbled to find the words to say. 'Knowledge of a thing is not necessarily possession of it, sir.'

'That's what it says. I know what it says,' roared back Dino. 'I asked you what you think it means.' His piercing eyes swung around the room again; a piece of shortened chalk poised in his strong fingers. Jaq wondered if he might throw it at the next person he asked.

'You…' Dino pointed at Martina.

'I think it means that you might know something but not necessarily be using it.'

'Precisely!'

Martina smirked, pleased that she had once again proven that she was a top-grade philosophy student.

And so, it went on. The lesson continued for what seemed to be an eternity. There was no fun, no laughter, no chaos, no chatting… just a prolonged session as Sir Dino fired one question after another at the next innocent victim.

*

'Aaaagh!' screamed Jaq throwing his school papers all over the floor. 'I can't do this!'

His mother's face appeared around the door. 'What is the matter?'

'This homework from Sir Dino. I can't do it and I must. Last week when Marco didn't complete it, he was made to clean out toilets after school.'

Mrs. Alfonsi sat down next to Jaq on the bed. 'Look, son, you're getting stressed. Don't panic. I am sure we will find something on the Internet.'

'Not even the Internet knows the answer. I spent all afternoon looking. It's just not fair! We were asked to find out who Franco Du Lupe was; but he simply doesn't exist.'

'Can I help?' Atalia's face appeared around the door.

'I don't think so,' sneered Jaq.

Mrs. Alfonsi ignored Jaq and beckoned Atalia in. 'You don't know anything about someone called Franco Du Lupe, do you, Atalia?'

'Yes', Atalia started with caution. 'He was a philosophy teacher. He developed some of his own ideas, but when he submitted them to the university, his ideas were mainly rejected and so he never got recognised for his philosophical thought…'

Jaq stared at her with disbelief. He almost thought for a moment that Atalia was making it up to trick him; but she continued for the next ten to twelve minutes so convincingly that he decided it was best to grab his notepad and pen and start scribbling it all down. Not even Martina would have been able to get all this information.

*

Back at school the next day, everyone walked into the Philosophy classroom with fear, not knowing the trouble that would befall them for 100% failure in completion of homework. Jaq decided that he would keep the information secret until the very last minute. Even Marco mustn't know, or everyone would be wanting to copy Jaq's work. He could have sold the answers to his friends and made some money, but the aggravation didn't seem it.

'I expect everyone failed with the homework,' declared Dino from the front. A smirk revealed that he hadn't expected anyone to complete the task. 'It goes to reveal that when studying philosophy, we can't always be expected to know the answers to everything.'

'But we can…' interrupted Jaq impatiently. 'I know who Franco Du Lupe was.'

'Very amusing, Jaq. Now, be silent,' replied Dino with an irritated expression on his face. He was not used to being interrupted.

'But I do, Sir…' interrupted Jaq again.

'Speak!' answered Dino, now contending for the fact that Jaq probably wouldn't be silenced until he had delivered some unlikely nonsense.

Jaq stood up. He didn't know why. It just felt like this was a moment of great significance. He cleared this throat and began to read out his notes. Marco's jaw just dropped whilst Martina glared at him with fury in her eyes. Once he had finished, there was silence, before Jaq decided he had better sit down again.

'I will see you at the end of class, Jaq,' answered Dino, and the rest of the lesson was spent learning about the thinking of Socrates and Plato.

When everyone had gone, Dino walked up to Jaq with a steely look in his eyes. 'Jaq, how did you find out this information?'

'My sister helped me, sir.'

'Is she at this school?'

'No, sir.' Jaq thought it best not to say anymore.

'I don't know how she knew this information. No-one should have known these facts. Franco Du Lupe was my father.'

Chapter 2

Mrs. Alfonsi, better known as Greta to the local village people, had married her husband, Giovanni, in 1991. As children they had both grown up together in the nearby city of Siena, attending the same school – although not in the same class – and whose parents were also good friends. It had not been a surprise to anyone who knew them when their engagement had been announced. They married soon after and relocated to San Gimignano where they could start life together as a married couple.

'Giovanni was so funny in his nature,' Greta had once told Atalia. 'He was a puppet maker and had once been employed making puppets of Pinocchio to sell in his uncle's little shop in Lucca. When he would take me out for the evening, he would have a miniature Pinocchio in his pocket and bring it out and dance it across the dining table in the restaurant. I would laugh, and everyone sat around would come and see what was going on.'

'So, what happened?' Atalia asked, trying to picture this man whom she imagined to be like Geppetto.

'Well, we got married and then Jaq was born. Giovanni was so proud. He had always wanted a son. Shortly afterwards, Giovanni became ill. His illness went on for years until just a few years ago he died.' A tear appeared in Greta's eye. 'He would have liked you though, Atalia.'

Atalia smiled and fetched a handkerchief for Greta to dry her eyes on.

*

It had all happened about fourteen months ago. Obviously living in a village like San Gimignano, and as typical with small Italian communities, everybody knows everybody. Greta Alfonsi hadn't imagined it was going to be any different a day than normal. Since Giovanni had died, her main responsibilities were to bring up Jaq and ensure that the sale of her homemade Mediterranean bread brought enough money into the home.

It was while she was making her next batch of dough, containing tomatoes, olives, onions and black pepper, that there was knock at the front door. Greta washed her hands and ran to see who was calling. The sight of Greta Alfonsi wearing her apron and covered in flour was not an usual one, particularly when she would need to dash out the house, across the street, and into the little shop that sold whichever ingredient she had temporarily run out of. This morning however, Carlotta stood at the door with a girl of about ten years old stood by her side. Greta invited them both in. Carlotta didn't wait for formalities but simply got straight to the point.

'Greta, this is Atalia.'

'Good morning, Atalia,' Greta replied. 'Are you visiting Carlotta?'

Atalia didn't answer.

'I am sure you will be very happy here, Atalia,' continued Carlotta. 'Since her poor husband died, Greta could do with some extra help around here. You will be the perfect person. She will look after you well.'

'Wait a minute,' replied Greta, looking slightly alarmed that Carlotta seemed to be pushing her agenda quite poignantly. 'Are you asking me if this girl lives here?'

'No, I'm not asking you that,' replied Carlotta. Greta sighed with relief. 'I'm telling you that,' replied Carlotta.

The sound of two Italian ladies debating with each other filled the street outside to a volume that any passing tourist might just think there was a full-blown row going on. Even Atalia had slipped out the front door and sat contentedly outside, waiting for an outcome.

'You can't leave her homeless wandering the streets of this village with nothing to eat, Greta. The poor girl was wandering around the towers in a world of her own up there. Not that she looked unhappy, mind you, and not that she has asked for anything since I came across her. All I am saying is that she needs someone and so do you, so that's final.'

Greta looked at Carlotta. She knew she was right; but the thought of having another child in the home had never even crossed her brain. Mind you, she thought, it might not be for long – just until we find her actual parents. It would be like fostering for a while. She could manage that, surely.

'Okay, Carlotta, she can stay.'

'Excellent.'

Carlotta didn't stay for much longer. Atalia had been brought back into the house and was quickly pushed into the bathroom to clean up whilst food was prepared for her in the kitchen.

When Jaq had arrived home from school, he was horrified to find a girl in the house.

'You mean, we're keeping her?' he queried.

'You make her sound like a pet,' replied Greta.

'But she's a girl…' Jaq protested.

Atalia looked at him. Clearly this was not going to be easy convincing Jaq that she was okay.

'Lazio and Fiorentina have been sent down to Serie B, where they will enter the championship with minus-seven and minus-12 points respectively,' Atalia started. She knew this was not the normal greeting when you meet someone for the first time; but she was confident that in the case of Jaq, this might just work and break down a few barriers instantly.

'Luciano Moggi, the Juventus general manager has been banned from football for five years and Franco Carraro has been excluded for 4½ years for failing to stop this rot at the very heart of the game,' she continued.

'What?!' replied Jaq, horrified at this outcome in the football scenario. 'I had better tell Marco straight away. See you later.'

With that, Jaq had run straight out the front door, calling Marco's name at the top of his voice – certainly loud enough for the entire village to hear.

'I think you'll get on together,' chuckled Greta. 'I didn't know you liked football.'

'I don't,' replied Atalia.

Greta's eyebrows raised and stared at her with both confusion and disbelief.

'Still, you are welcome here, Atalia.'

*

After a couple of weeks, Mrs. Alfonsi had decided that it was probably time to research the exact whereabouts of Atalia's parents. She had travelled by bus through to the city of Florence to enquire with the legal offices there.

The city was packed. An appointment had been made for 1pm, so Greta had decided that she and Atalia could spend some time enjoying the sites around the city first, starting with the costume gallery and the grounds of Palazzo Pitti as well as looking at all the amazing jewellery contained in its various cases. From there, they walked over the Ponte Vecchio, admiring all the gold jewellery in the store windows as they passed by; before going to see Florence Cathedral. There was no time to visit inside but its decorative façade and its orange-brown domes were impressive enough.

'Built by Arnolfo di Cambio and completed in 1434,' said Atalia in a matter of fact voice.

'Where did you read that?' Greta asked.

'I didn't. I just knew it,' replied Atalia, 'although this is the first time I have actually seen it in real life.'

Greta looked perplexed. This wasn't the first time that Atalia had come out with some detailed pieces of information and knowledge over the last couple of weeks. Although a quiet girl, Greta had observed, she certainly has a good brain in her head.

At 1pm, they arrived at the legal offices and were shown into a large room off to the right-hand side. An official clerk with a name badge reading 'Lorenzo' was sat behind the desk with a large set of papers and a computer in front of him.

'So, you're looking for the registered parents of this girl,' Lorenzo confirmed.

'Yes, sir.'

'What's the girl's name?' he asked.

'Atalia,' Mrs. Alfonsi replied.

'Atalia what?'

'I don't know,' replied Mrs. Alfonsi, looking slightly embarrassed that she had never thought to ask. Come to think of it, she didn't really know any personal information about Atalia at all, not even her age or date of birth. *I must look terribly rude,* thought Greta. *In fact, I must look terribly ignorant to the clerk here,* she continued in thought. The whole concept of being totally unprepared for this meeting hit her like a lightning bolt; but it was too late now. Atalia would have to speak for herself.

'My name is just Atalia.'

Lorenzo frowned, scratched his head and tapped something into his computer.

'What's your date of birth?'

Atalia looked down at the floor. 'I don't know.'

'Well, how old are you then?' enquired Lorenzo.

Atalia shuffled uncomfortably in her seat. 'I don't know that either.'

Lorenzo rubbed his chin with his hand and put his pen down.

'This isn't making my job very easy, miss,' he continued. 'What were the names of your parents?'

'I don't have any' Atalia answered. 'Not until now anyway or at least that's what Carlotta said.'

'Carlotta?' Lorenzo looked confused. His forehead was getting redder and he loosened his tie from around his neck and undid the top button of his shirt. He tapped some buttons on his computer which subsequently beeped back at him every few moments or so.

'Okay,' he sighed. 'Last resort. A fingerprint please.'

He took a fingerprint from Atalia, scanned it into his computer before resuming the tapping of more buttons.

'This,' he informed Greta, 'will give us her identity from birth. Every baby's fingerprint is registered on this international database. After that, we can start investigations to find her parents from birth certificates, etc., etc., etc.'

The computer made a loud beeping noise and a red box appeared across the screen. Lorenzo stared at it with disbelief. He started sweating profusely and got up from his chair to open a window before sitting down again.

'I don't know how to say this,' he stuttered to Greta. He paused. 'It's saying…' He paused again. 'It's saying, she doesn't exist…'

Chapter 3

Greta's Mediterranean bread-making had, over increasing months, become more and more profitable. This was largely because she now had Atalia's help both in producing the bread and getting it sold to the locals in the town; all of whom had taken a bit of a shine to Atalia and accepted her as one of the community. Many considered Atalia's arrival as a God-send after Greta's loss of her husband and they had noticed a new lease of life that Greta seemed to be experiencing.

'What about trying to sell your bread to the tourists?' Atalia had once suggested; but it had fallen on deaf ears. Greta believed that tourists bought ice-creams, postcards and souvenirs, not bread. Atalia however was not one to give up and felt that given the right approach and opportunity, the bread might indeed sell to tourists who hadn't yet had lunch and didn't want to sit down for a typical Italian meal of pasta or pizza.

'Please can we just try it?' she begged Greta.

Greta looked reluctant, but at the same time did not want to curb the enthusiasm of her latest adopted member of the family.

'Look, I shall give you a plate of samples. People never mind samples – particularly free ones. You can take the next loaf, cut it up into small pieces and pass it out on the street. See what response you get, but I am not making it a business.'

Atalia understood. She went upstairs to her bedroom, brushed her gingery-brown hair and changed into her 'Io amo l'Italia' (I love Italy) white t-shirt and black lycra shorts. Sunhat and sunglasses were necessary on a summer's day like today and a splattering of sun-cream.

Next, she found an old table, covered it with a bedsheet and wrote out a small sign that offered the passers-by 'out of this world Mediterranean bread'. It was a slight exaggeration, of course, but enough to still get people to taste the samples.

Those in the community who knew Greta well, smiled fondly at Atalia and obliged her worthy cause by taking a sample of the bread that they were all too well familiar with. Others came, took a sample and commented on what a talented baker Greta was. Then, from about 10am onwards, came the tourists.

Atalia watched and listened as they walked by, identifying which countries they were from either by their appearance, such as the Indian family of seven who didn't even stop for a sample of bread; or the German students whose unique accent made it clearly that they were on a residential language school camp.

Greta appeared outside on the street just before midday. The samples of bread were down to less than a dozen. She flopped down onto the old wooden bench next to Atalia, who by now was feeling a little tired from the hot sun.

A man, wearing an open neck shirt and a pair of corduroy trousers appeared at the table to take a sample. Unlike the others, he savoured the flavour of the bread in his mouth for quite a long time before swallowing it.

'Do you like it?' enquired Atalia, keen to learn of his reactions.

The gentlemen raised his hands and shrugged his shoulders. He thought and then said, Je ne parle pas italien. J'aime le pain - c'est délicieux. Moi aussi je suis boulanger de France'.

'C'est super. C'est Greta, la femme qui fait le pain,' replied Atalia. The man shook Greta's hand.

'What did he say?' Greta asked Atalia, slightly shocked at both the man's handshake and the fact that Atalia had communicated in another language.

'He was a French baker, Greta. He said that he liked your bread.'

Greta smiled. 'He is a good Frenchman,' she replied and wandered back into the house.

The fact that Atalia had spoken in French to the gentleman had made Greta curious as to what else Atalia knew that she didn't yet know about. By the end of that day, she had discovered (thanks to another set of bread samples) that Atalia was also fluent in

English, Spanish, Russian and Arabic to name just a few.

*

Jaq himself had been most appreciative to have a linguist living in the house. He himself was not fluent at learning languages and therefore felt that 'this girl' could easily do his homework for him. Atalia didn't quite see things in the same way. She was kind-hearted, yes, but doing work for somebody like Jaq who otherwise was going to put zero effort into it himself was not the deal. Eventually a compromise was reached and Atalia sat patiently at the table helping him with his English homework.

'You really are doing well with English, aren't you?' said Marco with an envious look in his eyes. 'You couldn't help me with this week's homework, could you?'

Jaq's expression of alarm nearly gave the game away, but Marco hadn't noticed. 'Err…no, I don't think so. We're very busy tonight, Marco. Sorry.'

'But I don't understand past perfect tense,' whined Marco.

'Neither do I,' replied Jaq, not thinking of what he was saying; before promptly laughing out loud and slapping Marco hard on the back to cover his mistake and make it look as if he was joking.

Marco clearly looked offended. His best friend was rejecting him. He was right to feel betrayed, after all they had been friends since they started walking – and surely if Jaq was so good at English, it wouldn't have taken much trouble to help him out, would it? Jaq's English grades had rocketed the last couple of months – not so much with speaking and listening, but certainly with reading and writing.

It was Greta's observance of Atalia's ability with speaking languages that prompted her to think about getting Atalia an education. Whilst she was a great help with making and selling the bread, it would be unfair for Atalia to not go to school and be educated for the future.

'But I don't need to go to school,' said Atalia. 'I know everything I need to know.'

'You need qualifications,' replied Greta quite adamantly. 'Baking bread is not the future for a young girl like you.'

The conversation continued for a few hours. Greta complimenting Atalia on her knowledge and wisdom but insisting that she passed some examinations. Atalia replying that examinations only produced a piece of paper (known as a certificate) so she didn't see much point. What difference would it make?

Greta however had decided that education was the best direction and so she applied for a place at the nearest British International School. This would enable

Atalia to get grades that would be recognised by Oxford and Cambridge.

*

The application had, of course, required an age and date of birth. Greta had deduced that Atalia must be about ten years old, judging by Oceana, the daughter of the milkman who lived further down the village. Her date of birth was determined by the day and month in which Carlotta had first brought Atalia to the house. It would be enough to satisfy the school to start with.

Jaq had, by all good reason, enquired why Atalia wasn't going to his school as it was so close by. Greta had replied that there were reasons he wouldn't understand and so the conversation never progressed any further.

*

Outside the British International School, Greta waved Atalia inside to sit her entrance examination. Inside there were children from all different nationalities and of different ages. Each one was there seeking a place at the prestigious school. One was wearing a sari; another in African attire; another boy wearing a shirt and tie – presumably British; and another wearing a kilt. Greta had insisted on buying a new outfit for Atalia. She had promptly chosen a white top, a green skirt and a red neck-a-chief. She was proud to be in Italy and was going to show it.

Shortly after, they were all escorted into a large hall, full of individual desks, where the examination would take place. The signage around indicated that many different examinations were taking place and that finishing times would vary. Atalia sat at the table and waited for the examination to start.

Ten minutes into the exam, she raised a hand and an invigilator came across to enquire as to the problem.

'This is too easy,' Atalia informed him.

'That's the paper you must do,' hissed the invigilator back; his face expressing annoyance that the enquiry had been inappropriate.

'But I've finished it,' replied Atalia, flicking through the pages.

The invigilator's face looked perplexed. He went to the front, spoke to another person and returned with a different paper. Atalia thanked him kindly for his help. She would not disturb him again.

This however was not true, and she promptly interrupted him another eight to ten times during the next hour and a half; each time giving him the completed examination paper and requesting another.

*

Greta stared at the letter from the British International School with disbelief. Atalia had been rejected. She read it and re-read it over and over. The examination results confirmed that Atalia was over-qualified. She had the academic ability of that of a university student in English, Maths, Reasoning, Science and Linguistics. It also commented that whilst she hadn't been tested for History, Geography, Music, Art, etc. she was more than likely over-qualified in those too. It recommended that they sought a Masters' Degree course in England.

'But… how did you do it?' asked Greta with total disbelief.

'The exams were just too easy,' replied Atalia frankly. 'I told you before… I don't need to go to school.'

'But how did you know all these things?' repeated Greta, still in a state of complete shock.

'I've been well taught,' replied Atalia. 'By the best, in fact…'

'By who?' insisted Greta.

'Not who,' answered Atalia. 'By experience,' and for the first time since arriving at the Alfonsi household, she wandered casually over to the piano, opened the lid, sat down and played Schumann's Toccata in C Major Op. 7

Chapter 4

The thought of a school trip had captured everyone's imaginations, particularly that of Jaq and Marco.

'I bet that we're going to watch a basketball tournament in Rome,' said Marco, whose brain never really ceased from thinking about the game. He was known for fitting basketball into every academic study where possible. Basketball League scores for Maths; basketball stadiums for Geography; pictures of basketball players for Art; and then various pieces of English writing all based on basketball –biographies of players; newspaper reports of tournaments; fiction writing about missing basketballs or players; persuasive arguments as to why you should play basketball; and so, the list went on and on.

'No, it's not,' replied Jaq. 'It's going to be a trip to the Palio Di Siena, watching the horses and riders compete. Have you ever seen it, Marco? It's amazing!'

'Sounds boring watching horse riders go around and around in circles,' replied Marco.

Jaq's face looked indignant. 'It's mostly definitely not,' he replied. 'You should see the action, the speed, the casualties, the blood…' he continued. 'Even if the jockey comes off the horse, the horse itself still competes. The jockeys keep whipping the horses to go as fast as they can. They can even whip the rival jockeys.'

Marco starred at him, disbelievingly. He had heard Jaq say a few crazy things in his time; but this was a classic. Whoever would allow a horse race in which the competitors whip each other.

Jaq insisted that it was true; and this conversation would have continued for a lot longer; but Martina interrupted, 'It's a philosophy trip remember, not a sports event.'

There was a moment of silence as the realisation that Marina's poignant truth meant that there was going to be no thrills, spills or chills with this trip.

'Anyhow,' Martina continued, 'wherever this trip is going to be, I know that I shall still be the best in the class. I know everything about philosophy. I was reading about Plato in bed last night.'

'That's a planet, isn't it?' taunted Jaq quite deliberately.

'Huh,' grunted Martina, turning her back on him and walking off with very deliberate footsteps, her black patent shoes clicking along the stone classroom floor.

Dino walked in a short while later. He was unusually casual, wearing a pair of blue cropped jeans, a yellow t-shirt, summer shoes and a sunhat. Around his neck hung a magnifying glass and a camera.

'Morning. Well, surprise, surprise – today's the day of the trip.'

'But we didn't know it was today,' protested Martina. 'I would have brought my camera, iPad and notebook if I had known. I need to go home and get them. I'll only be ten minutes.'

'No, you don't,' Dino replied. 'You come just as you are. This is a philosophy trip. All you need is your brain.'

Martina was going to argue that Dino had his camera, iPad and notebook but then decided that it was best to keep quiet and maintain her philosophical image and status.

*

There was no coach outside much to everyone's disappointment. 'We're walking,' Dino informed them, 'and we're not going far.'

'This is going to be boring,' whispered Marco in Jaq's ear.

'I wish he'd tell us where we're going,' replied Jaq. 'Just think though, if it's Alberto's Ice Cream Parlour, it could be exciting. I could become philosophical about ice-cream.'

Immediately Jaq went into his amateur dramatics mode in which he narrated an original skit in which the different flavoured ice-creams were reflecting on the poignancy of identity and purpose. Everyone was laughing as Jaq narrated the identity crisis of the mint chocolate chip ice-cream; when Dino stopped walking, turned around to Jaq and glared at him disapprovingly.

'This is not a comedy trip, Jaq,' started Dino, 'we are not going to the ice-cream parlour either. If you must know we are visiting the towers.'

'The towers...' everyone complained. 'We see them every day. We see them everywhere we go in the town. We see them from our bedroom windows. We're fed up to the teeth of the towers.'

'But have you looked at them philosophically?' asked Dino.

'Philosophically?! How do you look at some towers philosophically?!' thought Jaq.

Dino must have read his thoughts, or at least seen the frowned brow that said it all.

'Remember what Soren Kierkegaard once said, Life must be understood backwards but it must be lived forwards. Once you understand the philosophy of these towers then you will be able to move forward in life.'

Everyone thought it was the most absurdist statement they had heard from Dino to date, apart from Martina of course who professed to understand every word that Dino was saying.

'Well, explain it then,' said Chiara.

'No. I'll let you work it out,' replied Martina. 'It's not my fault if you're not as clever as me.'

Chiara mimicked Martina behind her back before promptly joining Jaq and Marco who she knew would protect her if there was an altercation.

*

There had originally been seventy-two towers in San Gimignano back in the fourteenth century. Jaq was rather relieved that there was now only thirteen as it was clear that Dino intended to examine each tower thoroughly. Each tower had been built by the rich and prosperous families in the town as a display of their wealth and status.

'A bit like the pictures of the modern day high rise buildings then,' suggested Jaq to Dino.

'In a way, yes,' replied Dino. 'Apart from the fact that it was competitive between the families.'

Dino stood on the first floor and continued taking photos, looking through his magnifying glass at various bits of stone wall, and mumbling to himself some philosophical quotes and thinking.

Jaq looked around. The rooms were quite small, some with the old stone steps leading from one floor to the next; others with wooden staircases specifically built to let visitors and tourists move from one level to the next. So far, he had deduced that originally when the towers were built, people had used them for different purposes. The main purpose had however been for domestic life. The information boards led him to believe that the ground floor was where the people of the day would carry out their working lives. The next floor would be for sleeping whilst the top floor would be for cooking.

'Seems a bit strange to go to the top floor for something to eat,' Jaq told Marco. 'Imagine if you wanted a secret midnight feast and you had to climb all these steps to the top without waking your parents up.'

'You'd get caught really easily,' replied Marco. 'I mean, imagine putting a kitchen upstairs in your house today. You'd creep up the stairs whilst all the time your mum is listening to the creaky floorboards above the bedroom ceiling. She would know it was you that had taken the last piece of pizza.'

'It's because…' interrupted Martina, 'if there was a fire, then the whole tower wouldn't burn down!'

Jaq and Marco looked at each other. Fair point, I suppose, thought Jaq. It might be easier to escape too.

'So… what are you thinking?' asked Dino, joining the conversation.

'Interesting,' said Jaq.

'Si,' added Marco.

'Boys, you are not getting it,' insisted Dino. 'You're looking at the history and geography of the towers. You need to think philosophically. What do these towers tell you about life, power, fame, position, destiny?'

'Errr…' started Jaq, having no idea how he was going to finish this sentence.

'I'll give you a clue. Try doing what I do,' and with that comment, Dino walked off.

The boys watched him. Dino was looking at the walls; staring at the floor; putting his ear to the walls; and muttering some philosophical quotes.

'He's bonkers,' said Jaq.

'Well, you heard what he said,' sneered Martina. 'Let's see you get philosophical, Jaq.'

'Hmmm…' mumbled Jaq. He went over to a wall, looked at it, stared at the floor, put his ear to the wall and then muttered the only philosophical quote he had remembered 'If life doesn't give you lemon and sugar, your lemonade is going to be terrible!' Perhaps not the most intelligent statement, but it would have to do for today.

Chapter 5

'It's 7pm, Atalia, wake up!' Jaq shoved Atalia's shoulder again. He needed to wake her up as dinner was just about to be served. He normally wouldn't have been too bothered and simply let his mother go crazy that someone was missing from the table; but they had visitors staying and Atalia's absence had already been noted. As far as Jaq was concerned, this was urgent. He had his own reasons for wanting this meal-time to go well. Eventually, Atalia stirred.

'She always has a long sleep in the afternoon, don't you, Atalia?' said Greta. Atalia didn't answer, but simply smiled at the people sat at the table to whom she had not yet been introduced.

'Hi Atalia. My name is Mr. Tonella,' the gentleman started. 'And this is my wife, Mrs. Tonella, and my daughter Alina.'

They greeted each other in the usual manner before heading towards the table to sit for dinner.

'You can sit here, Sir,' said Jaq, quickly pulling back a seat at the head of the table. 'You here, Mrs. Tonella,' he said, pulling out the next chair round the table in a clockwise direction. 'You here, Alina,' he said, beckoning Alina to the next chair.

Atalia went to sit next to Alina. She looks a little older than me, thought Atalia, but she seems pleasant enough.

'Not there,' said Jaq, his face looking both indignant and a little red, Atalia noted. 'That's my seat. You can sit next to Mama.' Atalia promptly moved to the seat between Greta and Mr. Tonella. There was little chance that she was going to be able to engage in any conversation at all with these two adults on either side of her, both of whom could talk continuously.

By contrast, Atalia noticed how closely Jaq had shuffled his chair up near to Alina and had a puppy dog look in his eyes. *Aaah*, thought Atalia, *someone's found a girlfriend!* She smiled across the table at Jaq who promptly shot her a glare back. Atalia got the message – better not wind Jaq up too much.

Jaq made himself the perfect host and Greta thanked him most deeply by the end of the meal; although none of the adults around the table had picked up any inclination as to the motive behind it all. Alina however had been most impressed and was seen wandering out the front door with Jaq, hand in hand; whilst the grown-ups retired to the living room for further conversation.

'I am so glad to be back in San Gimignano and to see you again, Greta,' said Mr. Tonella.

'So am I, Pietro,' replied Greta. 'You and your family are most welcome to come around any time.'

'It's good to meet you too, Atalia,' he said.

Atalia thanked him and then politely excused herself from the room. Clearly Greta and the Tonellas had plenty to catch up on, and it would be very boring to listen to their reminiscing.

'Are you going back to working on the archaeological dig?' she heard Greta ask Pietro.

'No, no, no…' laughed Pietro. 'I own a hotel now – the one at the bottom of the hill. Life has made me a rich man.'

The laughter spilled out again as Atalia closed the door.

*

Mr. and Mrs. Tonella left shortly after midnight. Atalia watched them go. It was interesting to note that Alina was not with them. Perhaps she had gone home earlier. There was one way to check. She went across the corridor and knocked on Jaq's bedroom door. There was no answer. She gently pushed it open and crept a few footsteps inside. This was forbidden territory and Atalia knew it. If Jaq was in his room, she would be yelled out and escorted out within seconds. Still there was no response. Jaq was clearly still out with Alina and life in the village was beginning to wind down to a close for the night.

She heard Greta go to bed, singing a little Puccini - 'O mio babbino caro…'; the song echoed through the house, but mainly out of tune. This was not unusual when a couple of bottles of Chianti had been downed before the solo act started. The song itself was normally beautiful, although be it sad; but Greta sang it as if the patriotism of Italy was at stake. She would deny even singing it in the morning.

Twelve thirty a.m. came and Atalia was in her pyjamas, sat up in bed, waiting. The frustration of Jaq not being home was causing great inconvenience. By 1 a.m. she could wait no longer. She crept out of her room and started to descend the stairs, making sure to avoid the one with the creaky floorboard.

She hadn't heard Jaq come in the door just moments before and both nearly screamed as they virtually collided round the bottom stair.

'Where have you been?' hissed Atalia.

'None of your business,' replied Jaq. 'What are you doing?'

'Oh,...um...I left something in the kitchen.' Atalia felt as if her mouth was struggling to utter a desperately needed excuse.

'Still hungry, I know,' said Jaq. 'Don't worry I won't tell if you won't.' He shot up the stairs with a smirk on his face.

Atalia continued creeping along the carpet, past the kitchen and to the back door. She hoped that Jaq wouldn't come back. It was unlikely, she reasoned. Jaq looked as if he had other things on his mind.

*

No more was said of the incident and it emerged that Jaq had been with Alina – the two of them, who hadn't known each other before – took to each other very quickly. Both now considered each other best friends and Jaq was regularly disappearing off in the evenings for a few hours at a time. He and Alina could regularly be seen walking through the village, hand in hand, eating ice-creams, laughing, chatting and generally milling around the place. The whole village soon knew that there was a young romance going on between the two of them. No-one encouraged it nor discouraged it. It was just a matter of fact.

*

'Mama, I think Atalia is having snacks during the night,' said Jaq.

'What makes you think that?' asked Greta, quite surprised.

'Well, on some occasions when I have got back late from being with you-know-who,' started Jaq. 'Atalia is quite often coming downstairs to the kitchen.'

Greta looked doubtful. Atalia certainly wasn't growing any tubbier. She wasn't growing any taller either, she noticed. *If Atalia was hungry, then she should just say something,* she thought.

It was a few days later that Greta asked Atalia whether she was eating enough. Atalia replied that she was most content with the food that she was getting.

'It's just that you seem to get very tired in the afternoons as well,' she enquired.

'I've always needed plenty of sleep,' replied Atalia, concerned that no-one should find out the truth of the situation. 'Don't worry about me, Greta. I am perfectly fine.'

No more questions fortunately. She would need to be more careful. It was clear that these subtle questions had the thoughts of Jaq behind them. She could no longer trust their passing-by on the stairs. She would have to ensure that Jaq was now in and asleep before slipping outside.

*

The weeks went by and the whole concern had passed over. In addition, Jaq and Alina had experienced a disagreement and so the late evening couple were no longer an item. Once again, the whole village knew of the split-up, but no-one commented. It was none of their business, and yet in Italy, everything is everybody's business.

For Atalia, this made life easier again. Jaq was now in bed asleep a lot earlier and she could easily creep down the stairs and out the back door. Greta was a deep sleeper so there was no chance of waking her.

All was going well until the night of the thunderstorm. Atalia had slipped out the back door at about half past midnight. About forty-five minutes later, there was a sudden crash of thunder causing the ground to vibrate. The lightning flashed violently, and the rain poured down in torrents. Atalia rushed into the house and tiptoed across the hallway and up the first few stairs. Jaq was standing at the top.

'Pssst! Where have you been? You're soaked!' he hissed.

Atalia's pyjamas were stuck to her body and her hair was leaving a trail of drips along the floor. She hurried into her bedroom, ignoring Jaq, and dried herself off as quickly as possible before closing the shutters and jumping into bed.

Greta never knew of the incident for whilst she had heard the storm; she hadn't realised that Atalia had been outside in it.

Atalia had been proactive in ensuring that her pyjamas were dry by getting them washed in the early hours of the morning and then putting them out on the balcony outside her bedroom to dry in the morning sun.

'So where were you last night?' Jaq insisted loudly at the dinner table. Greta turned and looked at Atalia.

'In bed,' replied Atalia. 'Where else would I have been?' she retorted.

'I seem to remember you looked a bit wet,' said Jaq, determined to get Atalia into trouble; but also, out of nosiness as to what she had been doing.

'Yes, I realised that's what happens when you leave the shutters open during a torrential rainstorm, Jaq.'

Jaq looked frustrated. Greta looked content with the answer. She suddenly turned and confronted Jaq which took both he and Atalia by surprise.

'Jaq. You leave Atalia alone. She doesn't need you snooping into her bedroom during the storm.'

'But I didn't,' protested Jaq.

'Then how did you know she was wet?'

'I passed her going to the bathroom,' said Jaq, looking quite embarrassed.

'Now, come on, Jaq, admit it, you were peeping round the bedroom door, weren't you?!' exclaimed Atalia, realising that Jaq would either run out of excuses or back down.

He glared back at her, got up from the table and announced that he was going to school.

*

'I'm telling you, Marco,' Jaq informed him, 'that girl is creeping downstairs and I don't know why.'

Marco looked disinterested. Jaq however continued labouring the point. 'I set up a booby-trap in the kitchen, but it never went off…' he continued.

'Why don't you just follow her?' enquired Marco.

'I can't,' answered Jaq. 'She only goes when I'm asleep. The only thing I have discovered however is that she creeps downstairs two times every night – once when everyone is asleep and again just before sunrise.'

The mystery of the girl in his house was getting deeper and deeper in Jaq's mind. He had a load of questions he wanted answers to:

Why didn't Atalia go to school?

What was the actual reason she was living with them?

What was she up to when she crept down the stairs twice a night in her pyjamas? And what was inside that bag that she always took down with her?

Chapter 6

It was Sunday morning. Although it was 9:30am, Jaq was lying in bed, pretending to be asleep. He had tried the same trick last weekend and it had worked in convincing his mother that he was over-tired. She would then leave him to catch up on more sleep whilst she and Atalia would go to Sunday Mass at the local church. Once they had gone, he would get himself up, eat breakfast, throw some clothes on and go out to meet up with Marco. Marco was always at home on a Sunday morning as his family were non-religious. He listened for the door to close; then crept over to the window and peeped out through the shutters, watching his mother and Atalia walk up the stony road to the Catholic Church. Good, they were gone.

It wasn't that Jaq had anything against religion. He believed in God and that, but he had grown weary of the Sunday morning Mass. By contrast, he knew that his mother had stuck to her religious tradition all her life; and seemingly Atalia had some sort of belief as well, although she never talked about it. *Come to think of it,* thought Jaq, *she doesn't really tell me anything unless she's helping me with my homework.* He contemplated on this thought for a few minutes, asking himself whether he should try and engage conversation with this girl that now lived in his house. The thought however passed quite quickly with a conclusion that he wouldn't bother. *What was the point? She might talk about girl-related things and nothing could be more tedious.* The only thing he did want to know, however, was the reason for the mysterious night walks.

*

'It's going to be difficult,' he explained to Marco. 'I need to find out why that girl gets up twice in the night.'

'Perhaps she's going to the bathroom...' replied Marco. 'That's what I do sometimes.'

'Oh, shut up,' answered Jaq. 'She doesn't go to the bathroom. She goes downstairs and out the back door.'

'To look at the stars?' suggested Marco, his eyes glinting as if a brainwave had just hit him.

'Twice every night?!' exclaimed Jaq.

Marco had to admit that it did seem a bit of a crazy idea. Like Jaq, he too could see no reason why anyone would get up twice every night and go out the back door.

'Perhaps she's got a pet and she doesn't want anyone to know about it, so she goes out there each night with food for it.'

Jaq's eyes lit up. 'Marco, you could be right! That's why she's got the bag with her. Marco, you are a genius.' He bowed Marco's head and kissed the top of it; then promptly wondered why he had carried out such an action. Marco was just as startled as Jaq, but simply rolled his eyes, ruffled his hair with his hands and kept staring at the tree blowing in the wind as if nothing had happened.

*

Jaq knew he had to do something. If he followed Atalia, she would hear him and subsequently confront him. She would then be on watch out for him every night and so he wouldn't find out anything. *No*, he thought, *it must be subtler than that.*

He sat outside on the doorstep, watching the tourists go by, pondering over a plan. *He could just ask her, but he knew that she wouldn't tell him anything.*

'Scusi,' came a voice from in front of him. Jaq looked up. There was a couple in their twenties stood in front of him, holding out a camera. The man was gesticulating about taking a photo. Realising that the couple clearly wanted their picture taken (and having an inability to speak Italian), Jaq nodded, held the camera and promptly took their photo. The couple took the camera back, looked at the picture, smiled and then gave him a thumb up. 'Grazie'.

The incident of the photo would have passed by without any further consideration, but it had given Jaq an idea – *what if he could get a photo of the pet that Atalia was looking after? Even better, what if he filmed Atalia going out to see her pet. He imagined her going outside with a bag of food only to find a monkey hidden behind a tree who then would come scampering out to see her. Atalia would have her finger on her lip, telling the monkey to be quiet in case he or his mother heard them.*

His imaginations were interrupted by Greta appearing on the doorstep with a plate of food in her hand. It was lunchtime and she was tempting him in with the delicious smell of a bacon and gorgonzola pasta. It was a favourite of Jaq's and so he submitted himself readily and was soon consuming it faster than a monkey with a banana.

*

By the time it was midnight, Jaq had conceived many different ideas as to what Atalia's pet could be. *He was convinced that a pet was the reason she took her bag with her. Not only that, but it was also why Atalia didn't go to school. She and his mother were clearly both in on the secret. But tonight, everything was going to change. He was going to know the truth.*

He slipped into his black pyjamas and socks before creeping down the stairs to the back door. Here, he found his black flip-flops which he had conveniently situated earlier that evening. He opened the back door, crept out, and slowly closed the door behind him.

It was a dark night. The moon was hidden behind cloud and the occasional streetlamps were too far away to bring any light into the back garden. He looked around, trying to find somewhere to hide. Behind the large terracotta pots holding the bay trees in would be best. From there, Jaq positioned his iPad. He would film the incident. This would give him evidence that he could show his mother if she didn't already know.

He waited and waited for what seemed like ages. Eventually, the back door opened and Atalia stepped out into the garden, carrying the green bag with the coloured zips over her shoulder.

'Okay, here goes,' thought Jaq, starting the iPad in its camera recording mode.

Atalia went to the corner of the garden not far from where he was hiding. Jaq realised that he would need to remain very still as to not get discovered. He certainly wouldn't want Atalia to think that there was a stranger in the garden and then wake up his mother. He would be grounded for certain.

Atalia sat down, crossed her legs and started to unzip her bag. Jaq couldn't see what it was she was getting out of her bag, but she seemed to be putting a lot of things on the ground – presumably the food for whichever animal was about to make its appearance.

The next half an hour was utterly boring. No animal appeared. No great action took place. He just watched as Atalia seemingly just sat motionless. Eventually she put whatever-it-was back in her bag, zipped it up and walked back into the house, locking the back door behind her.

'Damn!' uttered Jaq. 'I am locked out.' He contemplated his options – *climb the wall into next door's garden?* No, they would think he was a burglar. He would normally have climbed the guttering but that led up to Atalia's bedroom window and if she realised he was in the garden the whole plan would be blown. There was nothing else for it. He would have to stay where he was until Atalia came back out again later. He would then have to try and creep in unnoticed.

*

'You look very tired,' commented Greta over the breakfast table the next morning.

Jaq yawned. His eyes were bloodshot, and his body ached all over from hiding / sleeping behind a terracotta pot for nearly four hours before Atalia had come back out again and he had managed to creep back inside. As far as he was aware, Atalia had no knowledge of his presence in the garden last night.

'Bad night's sleep,' he replied. 'I couldn't get comfortable.'

Atalia walked into the room. 'Morning,' she greeted them before walking over to the kitchen cupboard and fetching a croissant, some cheese, ham and grapes.

Jaq stared at her. It was this girl that had given him such a bad night. It was her fault that he had spent hours huddled up behind a terracotta pot, trying to get some sleep. *She shouldn't have keys*, thought Jaq. *She isn't a proper member of the family.*

'Can I stay home from school today, Mama?' he said. 'I don't think I feel well.'

'You don't look too good,' answered Greta. 'But school is only until lunchtime, so you can sleep this afternoon.'

It was a good attempt to get out of school, thought Jaq. He glared at Atalia again, envious that she didn't go to school for reasons he had still yet to discover.

*

When the afternoon came, Jaq went to bed. He was supposed to be sleeping and nearly dropped off immediately, but there was one thing he wanted to do first. He switched on the iPad and found the video clip he had taken the night before. He watched as Atalia had come out of the back door and into the garden. She had sat down, opened her bag and was taking some things out of it and putting them on the floor. Jaq paused the video, snapshotted it and zoomed in to see what they were.

What he saw made no sense. There were twelve stones which Atalia had positioned one by one in a circle, much like the numbers on a clock. Then there were two sticks, one longer than the other. The first pointed north and south; the other east and west but with the stick pointing at what would be stone two and stone ten. Atalia had then sat there with her palms on her lap, one on top of the other. *What was she doing?* He played the video again and again, looking for every little detail.

It was only on the twenty third time of watching that he noticed that Atalia's lips were moving. *She was saying something.* He turned the volume to try and hear, but it was in a language he didn't understand. Still, not a problem, he would simply use the Internet interpreter app to decipher the words.

The sticks and stones seemed irrelevant now. The important thing was the words. The app started. Jaq uploaded the video. In the next few seconds he would know what Atalia was saying. Not only that, but he would know which language (out of the world's six thousand, five hundred) she was speaking and that might give some clues as to where she can come from in the first place.

The 'Please wait for a moment' message seemed to stay on the screen for ages. There was a beep. This was it. The result he had been looking for... but no, he couldn't believe his eyes. Surely this couldn't be true. There was just two words. In big bold, red letters, the words appeared 'Language Unknown'.

*

Chapter 7

'Atalia, how many languages can you speak?' blurted out Jaq at the breakfast table the next morning.

'Just a few,' replied Atalia casually, having no idea of why Jaq would ask such an unusual question. 'Do you need help with some homework or something?'

'Err, no… I just wondered that's all.'

Atalia reeled off a few simple greetings in French, English, Russian and Spanish. Jaq looked impressed, but he was still puzzling over how to find out what language Atalia had been speaking in the video recording.

'Do you know any unusual languages?' Jaq persisted.

Atalia frowned and shook her head. 'No… I don't think so.' Deep inside, Atalia knew that there were many other languages that she knew fluently, but she wasn't prepared for Jaq to know everything about her. Besides she had no reason to trust him with personal information.

'Why all the sudden interest in languages?' asked Mrs. Alfonsi, carrying the freshly baked bread out of the oven and onto the breakfast table. 'Are you planning to become a linguist, Jaq?'

'Not likely,' retorted Jaq. 'I would hate having to keep translating all the time. I can't think of anything more boring.'

Atalia got up from the table, cleared her breakfast items to the old stone sink and proceeded to walk towards the door. 'I'll see you later, Mama,' she said.

'Mama', thought Mrs. Alfonsi. She had never heard Atalia call her Mama before. It seemed kind of touching and the surprise of it kept her motionless for a few seconds.

'Can languages be created?' asked Jaq to his mother.

'Jaq! What is it with you and languages today?' exclaimed Mrs. Alfonsi. 'Go and make up a language if you're that keen. Just don't use it to anyone in the village – keep it to yourself – we're don't want the community thinking that you've gone out of your mind.'

Jaq walked out the door, contemplating the idea and wondering if that was exactly what Atalia had done – made up a language. *It would make sense because, in that way, she would be the only person to understand it. Yet Atalia seemed to be a more intelligent person than to make up a nonsense language. No, there was something more to it than that. He would just have to wait until the right moment to find out more.*

*

'Right,' said Mr. Dino from the front of the class. 'Get your clipboards and pencils. We're having another lesson outside of school today.'

The class whooped in excitement. 'Where are we going this time?'

'Just wait and see, but don't get too excited.'

Once again, eager voices quickly chattered away, speculating where they would be going to this time. Marco was convinced that this time it had to be a baseball match. Jaq reminded him that baseball wasn't exactly a leading sport in Italy.

When Dino appeared again he was carrying some historical documents and some maps. It was difficult to see anything from the way that they were folded under his arm, but they gave the impression of looking pretty boring.

'Now remember,…' Dino boomed, 'we are looking for philosophical reasons behind why people do what they do. Today, I am taking you to the heart of the most dangerous and criminal minds.'

'Alcatraz,' blurted out Marco.

'I don't want to go to Alcatraz,' sobbed little Ginsella. 'I want to go home. I don't want to come.'

'Don't be stupid, Ginsella,' replied Dino. 'We're not going to Alcatraz. What a stupid thing to say, Marco. See me after school today for detention.'

Marco hung his head down whilst Jaq shot one of those 'could have told you' looks across at him.

*

Ten minutes later the class, led by Dino, were walking through the heart of San Gimignano, not really paying any particular attention to where they were going until Dino suddenly stopped and pointed at the tallest tower in the town.

'That,' he declared 'is where we are going.'

'What?!' replied Jaq who happened to be stood right behind Dino. 'We went to the towers last time.'

'Yes, but this time you are only going to the one tower. It's called the Devil's tower.'

'I'm scared,' whimpered Ginsella. 'What if he gets me?'

'He doesn't exist,' answered Antonio. 'He's just a figment of the imagination.'

'True,' said Dino, 'but someone named it the devil's tower for a reason and that's what we are going to find out. What was the philosophical reason behind it?'

*

Dino had the class looking amongst all the stones, floors and walls for clues as to why this tower had been called the Devil's Tower. Jaq had wondered why they hadn't just looked up the information on the Internet. *Surely this would have been much easier than spend ages staring at old bits of stone.* It was only a short time before the class left the tower that a different philosophical question hit Jaq's mind. *Why was Dino so interested in the class looking at the tower? Why hadn't he just asked them to look up the historical records?*

The more Jaq thought about it, the more curious he became. *Dino definitely had an unusual interest in the towers. This had been their second visit to the towers in the same term. Not only that, but Dino had recently talked rather a lot about the towers in his lessons.* He also remembered that there was now a picture behind Dino's desk in the classroom of the towers, particularly of the one they had visited today – the Devil's tower.

'Marco, you have to help me,' said Jaq. 'Dino seems besotted with the towers. There must be a reason behind why he finds them so interesting.'

'Perhaps he just likes history,' suggested Marco.

'No, Marco,' replied Jaq. 'There's more. Remember, each time we go to visit them, he always reminds us that we are looking at the philosophy, not the history.'

'I don't get it though,' said Marco. 'How would these towers be philosophical?'

'I don't know,' answered Jaq. 'But clearly Dino thinks there is. We need to try and figure out what he is thinking.'

*

'Mama, can Marco and I go to Dino's house?'

'What do you want to disturb your teacher for? The man needs a break from you lot. Besides which it is getting dark and it's only an hour to your bedtime.'

'Please,' whined Marco and Jaq together. 'We want to ask if he will consider running a study group one evening.'

'A study group?!' Mrs. Alfonsi nearly fell over backwards in surprise. 'You two want to do more study?'

Marco and Jaq looked at each other with a pretence look of innocence on their faces. *If they could just go to Dino's and get him to start talking about the towers, he might just let some information slip.*

'Yes, we need to revise our philosophy before the mid-year examinations,' answered Jaq, desperately hoping his mother would believe him.

'Oh, go on then...' replied Mrs. Alfonsi, 'just don't blame me if he sends you away with a good telling off for disturbing him.'

*

Dino's wife answered the door. Marco and Jaq had never seen her before so didn't quite know how to greet her. 'Excuse me, could we see Dino please? It's very important.'

'No, you can't – he's out walking,' came an abrupt reply before the door closed immediately with no further opportunity to enquire as to where Dino might have gone.

'I bet I know where he is,' said Jaq. 'I reckon he's up at the towers.'

'But it's getting dark and it's creepy up there,' whispered Marco.

'Don't be such a baby,' hissed Jaq. 'Come on, we will just go and look at the entrance of the devil's tower. If Dino is going to be anywhere, he'll be at that tower.'

The two boys walked through the town towards the tower. As they drew near to the entrance to the devil's tower, all was silent. They looked behind them and then took one footstep inside the door.

It was dark and gloomy. The old stone walls seemed to be mysteriously eerie and the bearers of some old time secrets yet to be spoken. The air was thick and the moonlight hidden behind some heavy cloud.

Suddenly there was the sound of footsteps coming towards them. 'Quick, hide,' said Marco.

They dashed behind the nearest building and watched to see who would emerge from the tower. A man wearing a long black coat and a black hat appeared in the doorway. He looked left and right before slipping out into the night. An owl hooted, and the man ran, dropping something accidently out of his pocket. The boys watched him go before tiptoeing over to look at the item the man had dropped. It was a map – a map showing the building construction of the tower.

*

In class, the next day, Dino did not seem his usual self. He seemed perplexed, perturbed and troubled by something.

'Is everything okay, sir?' asked Jaq politely.

'Umm… well, yes, umm.. no actually. I've lost an important piece of paper.'

'What does it look like?' asked Marco innocently.

'I can't tell you,' snapped Dino. 'It's confidential information.'

'It wouldn't be this one, would it?' enquired Jaq, pulling the map out of his pocket. 'We found it last night.'

'Yes! That's the one,' exclaimed Dino, his face lighting up as if he had just won the national lottery. 'Where did you find it, boys?'

'Just outside the Devil's tower last night,' answered Jaq.

'Well thank you very much, boys. You have saved me a lot of trouble. I don't know how it got there.'

'No idea ourselves,' said Jaq, determined that Dino shouldn't know that they had seen him the night before.

'No,...no idea...' continued Marco. 'Perhaps you dropped it when you were on your way home... or when an owl hooted or something like that!'

Jaq glared at Marco and they started heading for the classroom door. Dino looked as if he was simply in a daze. As the boys left the room, his mind suddenly clicked onto something Marco had said. *'Or when an owl hooted or something'. That was exactly what had happened.* He pondered for a moment. *Perhaps the two boys had seen him. He couldn't be sure. Was the statement coincidence or had they been there? There was only one thing for it. He needed to be more careful next time.*

Chapter 8

No-one had imagined that Greta Alfonsi would have an accident. She was always so careful and aware of dangers that existed – often warning other people to be careful, particularly if they were well advanced in years or had a disability.

'It is our God-given duty to care for all people, regardless of their age or circumstances,' she would say when others looked reluctant to help out. 'You can't refute it – even the Pope agrees with me.' This always brought a smile to peoples' faces as they knew too well that Greta and the Pope had never met – nor were they likely to – but the idea that Greta could put the Pope into place with her thinking and ideas was not an inconceivable fantasy.

'The world would be a very different place if you ran it, Greta,' Antonio, the vinedresser, had once said. Atalia hadn't stayed around to hear the next part of the conversation. Antonio had a reputation for talking. If he had only used his words for writing instead of speaking, he could have gone on to be a successful author; but that was not Antonio's dream. Simply growing grapes to sell at the market was as much as he desired in life.

*

Jaq was not at school. The holidays had begun, and he was enjoying time wandering around with Marco talking about sport and spending hours in the old basketball court throwing a ball up and down. Greta had asked him once or twice to do a few errands around the town which subsequently got forgotten, resulting in Atalia doing the jobs for him. Atalia didn't mind however. She felt at home in San Gimignano and pretty much knew everybody on first name terms. Likewise, no-one really considered Atalia to be anything but Greta's daughter. It was if Atalia had always been there.

When eight o clock in the evening came, Jaq would reappear in the house. Greta had always said that Jaq's stomach was his alarm clock and so Jaq could always be relied upon to be in the house when the dinner was about to be served onto the table. Today was no different. Greta had just finished cooking some chicken, tomatoes and pasta as well as preparing some gorgonzola and herbs.

'Atalia, keep an eye on the dinner whilst I just go get the laundry in.' She fumbled around for the old wicker basket that she always carried the washing around in. On finding it, Greta wandered out the kitchen door and started going up the stairs.

'Jaq!' yelled Atalia.

Jaq jumped to his feet from off the sofa in the living room. He had never heard Atalia yell so loud and instantly thought something had gone wrong. Whilst

Jaq was not always the most helpful of sons, he could be a very considerate boy when he thought that someone was in trouble or danger.

'What's the matter?!' he said, running into the kitchen and seeing Atalia just stood next to the stove, stirring the dinner.

'Get the sofa cushions and put outside the kitchen window.'

'But that's on the street!' Jaq protested. 'Mama will kill me.'

'Just do it – and don't ask questions. Quick – it's urgent!'

Jaq sensed that there was no point arguing. There seemed no point putting the sofa cushions out on the street either, but he went and did it all the same. He had never seen Atalia in such a directive mood – and the idea of questioning her authoritative tone just didn't go through his mind.

He grabbed the sofa cushions, one under each arm and one in each hand – opened the front door and lay them side by side just by the kitchen window.

'What now?' he said, as he came back into the kitchen.

From above them, there was a loud cry followed by a heavy thump outside.

'That's what!' said Atalia.

Jaq rushed out the door to see his mother sprawled on the sofa cushions. He knelt down next to her and wrapped his arms around her. 'I'm here, Mama,' he said.

Atalia turned the stove off and also came out to see what assistance she could offer.

'She must have fallen off the balcony,' said Jaq, removing the surrounding laundry that was strewn across the walkway. 'Atalia take this washing inside before it all gets ruined. I'll try and see to Mama.'

'I'm okay, Jaq...' said Greta weakly, clearly very shaken up from the fall.

Jaq looked up at the second floor. The balcony bars had broken. Greta must have leaned against them when she was bringing the washing in on the pulley that went between their house and the one opposite. Subsequently she had fallen, but fortunately landed on the sofa cushions.

By now the locals had gathered around, having heard Greta's cry, and seeing her lying on the floor. All of them were asking whether she was okay and if an ambulance was needed. Jaq said that he didn't know but they should wait until they had a better idea of what state his mother was in.

After what felt like ages, but, in reality, was probably about a quarter of an hour or so, Greta tried to sit up. She had no cuts or bruises, but clearly was suffering from shock. Her ankle seemed a little swollen and as she got up to walk, she found it was painful to put weight through. Atalia went under one arm whilst Jaq went under another whilst other people went ahead or behind to assist in getting Greta into the house. Antonio had picked up the sofa cushions, pushing ahead into the house to put them back on the sofa for Greta to lay on them again. No-one seemed to even question how the sofa cushions had got out there in the first place.

Greta lay on the sofa, shocked by her own mishap and totally unfamiliar with injury and accident. Sure, she had seen enough people do things in her time, but she never had, and this experience was proving to be a first. Hopefully, it would be her only one, she thought.

By 9:20pm, Atalia had returned to the stove in the kitchen and served up the re-heated dinner that had been prepared earlier that evening. Jaq ate his meal so rapidly that anyone would have wondered if he had eaten in the last week or two. Greta, by contrast, took a few steady mouthfuls before declining any more. Atalia watched her, considering her progress and looking for any signs that Greta might need her to do something.

It wasn't long after that Greta decided that she would sleep on the sofa for the night and see how she felt in the morning. If necessary, she would send for the doctor then – but she considered it unlikely.

Jaq, of his own initiative, washed up all the dirty plates and pans following the meal and actually proved himself to be quite helpful. Atalia thanked him for his assistance before fetching some sheets for Greta to use for her sofa-bed.

'Atalia?' Jaq called out before going into his own bedroom for the night. 'You knew Mama was going to fall, didn't you? That's why you asked me to get the sofa cushions put outside the window.'

'I saw that it was going to happen,' replied Atalia in a quiet, matter-of-fact way.

'But how?' enquired Jaq. 'How did you know?'

Atalia thought hard for a second. *This was a difficult moment and needed to be handled carefully.* 'I think it's because I had seen how old the balcony was getting.'

Jaq pondered this response. 'I agree,' he said after a while. 'But that still doesn't explain how you knew that it would be today that Mama would fall.'

Atalia looked at him, smiled and said 'goodnight, Jaq' as she walked into her own bedroom and closed the door. Jaq stood on the landing not knowing what to think. Eventually he wandered into his own room, lay on his bed, staring at the ceiling, and wondering what kind of step-sister he really did have after all.

*

Greta seemed a lot better in the morning and had clearly got over the shock of what had happened. Frosino, the ironmonger, had come to the house at about 8:15am and promised to repair the balcony immediately at no cost. 'We look after each other in this town, Greta,' he said – his little black moustache twitching with every word that he uttered. 'I shall be finished by lunchtime – no problem.'

Greta thanked him very much and Jaq went to watch Frosino at work.

In the meantime, Greta was inundated with visitors from all over the town. Her ankle was now in a support and she could put a little weight through it, but after a few steps she needed to sit down again.

Atalia had got up early to help Greta get washed and dressed before going into the kitchen to make the bread.

'Forget the bread,' Greta had called out. 'They can do without it for one day. Tomorrow I shall be back to normal.'

Perhaps, Atalia thought, *this was why Greta had received so many visitors. They all wanted to know what had happened to their bread orders*; but Atalia was wrong – no-one seemed to care about the bread. They were there to see Greta – to talk, chat, ask questions and go through the event over and over again. Greta kept explaining to each one of them about how she had gone to get the washing in, leaned over the balcony which had collapsed in front of her. She had fallen from the second floor but fortunately landed on the cushions on the pavement. At this point, she would make the sign of the cross and thank God that she hadn't suffered a far worse injury.

Greta's visitors left one by one and went and told other people in the town what she had said – each one of them embellishing one or two details of the story as they went; so that by the time Greta's brother arrived from Pisa, the story had completed altered. Gossip now had it that Greta had been planning to somersault off the balcony on the second floor onto the cushions on the street below, and that the initial somersault had gone well, but that she had landed too heavily on her ankle and therefore it was injured for a while.

Atalia simply raised her eyebrows, amazed at the literary creativity of the people around her. *Talk about lying. No-one would ever have called it lying however, just exaggerated truth. There was no harm in that, was there?* Atalia wasn't sure she could agree. Surely truth was truth and that's all there was to it.

*

It took about a week before Mr. Dino, the school teacher arrived at the house. Jaq hid in his room, troubled as to why his philosophy teacher had come around.

'Rumour has it, Mrs. Alfonsi…' Dino started, 'that you were going to do a somersault off the balcony. With no offence, dear lady, but you don't give me the impression that it's the kind of thing you would do.'

Atalia, who was listening from behind the door, smirked. She knew that Mr. Dino was thinking about Greta's build which was a little larger than the average Italian woman.

'So, what exactly did happen?' Dino continued. 'I hope you don't mind me asking, but I am a philosophy teacher and therefore like answers to questions I don't understand.'

'I fell,' replied Greta. 'There's no more to it than that.'

'Oh…' said Dino, his face turning quite downward. He paused for a moment. 'In that case, what were the cushions doing lying on the street?'

Greta stopped and considered the question. It hadn't once crossed her mind. What were her lovely sofa cushions doing on the street?

'I don't know,' she replied. 'I shall ask Jaq when I see him. You know what boys are like, Mr. Dino.'

'Indeed, I do, Mrs. Alfonsi. I won't hold you up any further though. I am sure you want to rest.'

'Thank you, Dino,' said Greta. 'Please close the front door behind you.' With that, Dino left the house.

Jaq, hearing the front door closed, gazed out the window to see his philosophy teacher walking thoughtfully down the street.

'What did he want, Mama?' he said, walking into the living room where Greta was resting on the sofa with her foot up on the old, red pouffe.

'He wanted to know how and why the sofa cushions ended up on the street before I fell,' replied Greta curiously.

'I don't know,' replied Jaq, trying to look as innocent as possible. 'Perhaps you should ask Atalia.'

'Perhaps I shall,' replied Greta thoughtfully, knowing that if Atalia had anything to do with it, there was reason. *Atalia never did anything without a reason behind it* – Greta knew that for sure. Besides which Greta knew that had it not been for the cushions, the outcome could have been a lot more disastrous. 'Perhaps I shall ask Atalia,' she repeated. 'Perhaps I shall.'

Chapter 9

Greta recovered quite quickly and soon the matter of the fall was totally forgotten about. 'Today's news always becomes tomorrow's rubbish' said Greta, who never cared for reading papers or watching television, but was more than happy to listen to the local chitter-chatter.

Atalia was somewhat relieved that no-one mentioned the subject of the sofa cushions and was content that even Jaq hadn't asked about it for a couple of weeks. School was going to resume shortly so that meant Jaq would be back to studying. Atalia therefore was confident that life was going to go back to normal, if not slightly quieter as the summer tourists started to go home.

*

When Jaq came home from school on the first day of the new academic year, his face looked as white as a ghost and he was holding a pile of books in his hands. He dropped them onto the table with a thud, let out a long sigh, before slumping himself on the kitchen chair and putting his head into his hands.

'What's up, son?' Greta asked him concerned.

'This…' replied Jaq with a tone of disbelief in his voice. 'This is this year's books. Can you believe it? I mean, how I am going to possibly learn all this lot. It will take me decades… and half of these I don't actually want to read. Look!'

He pointed at a couple of titles with great frustration. 'The history of Italian architecture; The fall and rise of the Roman Empire; Palaeontology…I mean, what is that?'

'Palaeontology is the study of human life based on fossils,' replied Atalia who had been listening from across the other side of the kitchen. 'It's quite interesting actually, particularly when you look at the arguments for how the dinosaurs became extinct.'

'What do I care for how the dinosaurs snuffed it?' retorted Jaq.

'Calm down, Jaq' said Greta. 'There's no point getting yourself all worked up. You know how it is – the work has to get done. If you want to be successful in life, you have to work and study hard.'

'I'd rather learn about sport,' replied Jaq, picking up his books and dragging himself upstairs.

*

It wasn't long before Atalia was requisitioned for helping Jaq with his homework. On one hand, Jaq begrudged her help, but he knew that without her, the work would be pretty impossible – and actually his grades were going up quite nicely. *Thankfully*, he told himself, *most of his results would be coursework related and therefore there was no great need to learn too much for the exams next summer. Even if he didn't do well, the coursework would still make up 75% of his overall grade. With Atalia's knowledge, he was on his way up the ladder of success.*

Atalia didn't seem to mind either. Her concern for the welfare and best of others was a significant priority in her life. 'I'm simply giving out from that which I have,' she told Greta when Jaq had given Atalia quite a hard time over a particularly tricky piece of homework. Greta nodded and thanked Atalia for helping Jaq, knowing that she would get nothing in return from Jaq who simply grunted when the work was all done.

*

It was one Friday morning during a philosophy lesson that Jaq stumbled upon something that confused him. He had asked if he could leave the class to go to the toilet and eventually Mr. Dino let him go, but only after giving a long speech about how human beings could or should determine the right time and occasions to do (or not do) certain things. Jaq felt like telling him that this wasn't the right time to give a speech, particularly as he was so desperate, but he decided not to in case Mr. Dino gave another encore.

On his way back to class, the secretary asked Jaq if he could take a letter to Dino that had arrived in the post that morning. Jaq shrugged his shoulders and said that he didn't mind. He took the envelope and started off back to class.

Just before reaching the classroom door, Jaq took a quick look at the writing on the envelope. It was messy and rather wiry in its appearance. The school address looked alright, but Dino's name didn't look right. Jaq dashed back to the toilets to take a closer look at it behind the locked door of a cubicle. By holding it up to the window light behind him, Jaq could make out the letters D.I.N.O. for the first name; but the surname was certainly not 'Du Lupe' as Jaq had suspected after the incident with the homework last year. It read 'Salvucci'. *How strange*, Jaq thought.

He arrived back in the classroom and handed the letter to Dino who simply took it, read the envelope, opened it up, read it to himself, smiled and put it back into the envelope. Jaq never saw the letter again.

'I tell you, Marco,' said Jaq at lunchtime. 'Dino's surname is Salvucci.'

'Let's check on the staff photo board at the front of the school,' suggested Marco.

'Great idea!'

Both boys rushed off nearly knocking a playground supervisor over in the process. They walked past the principal's office and over to the board.

'Mr. Dino Du Lupe' read Marco with a confused look on his face.

'So, I was right!' exclaimed Jaq. 'He is Mr. Du Lupe.'

'Or is he?' asked Marco. 'Maybe he's not Mr. Du Lupe – maybe he's only pretending to be Mr. Du Lupe.'

'That could mean that his name is really Mr. Salvucci,' added Jaq. 'The problem is, how are we going to find out the truth?'

'Well…he didn't comment about the envelope, did he?' said Marco.

'No, that's true, he didn't. Let's assume therefore that Mr. Salvucci is his real name. After all, the secretary knew who he was – she asked me to give him the envelope.'

Both boys stood mulling over the problem until the school bell rang so loudly above them that they decided they had better move quite quickly so as to avoid the principal who would at any moment come out of his office.

*

The matter remained a mystery for quite a few weeks and neither Marco nor Jaq could think of anyway to find the answer to the problem without directly asking Mr. Dino for themselves. Being a philosophy teacher, they suspected that Dino would have a rather long, drawn-out answer anyway. The problem only became more of a mystery when Jaq was set another impossible piece of homework for history.

Jaq's history teacher didn't believe in anything being done half hearted. If you were asked to do something, you were expected to do it to the very best of your ability. Research was to be thorough and all information to be as accurate as possible, giving all details of where you had found the information in the bibliography. Jaq had once been tempted to just write Atalia's name down in this section, but then decided that it was probably not diplomatic and could cause some difficult explaining to do.

The homework was connected to the study of Italian architecture. So far, Jaq had been learning about the work of Michelangelo, including a marble sculpture of David created during the 16th Century. The statue, which stood just over five metres high, could be found in the Galleria dell'Accademia in Florence. Jaq was hoping that at some time, there would be a school trip to see Michelangelo's work particularly as Florence wasn't too far away from San Gimignano.

This time however the homework was to look at architectural buildings from around about the 13th Century. As Jaq worked with Atalia in studying this information out, it became apparent that the towers in San Gimignano had been built during this time. This was clearly the result that the history teacher had been hoping they would discover; but something else caught Jaq's attention that would result in a lot more research being done.

The information on the page in front of him read as follows:

When the towers of San Gimignano were built, they cost a lot of money. This was because the materials were expensive, and the workers needed to be paid. Only rich people could afford for them to be built and each one wanted to make their tower higher than the others, so they could prove themselves to be the wealthiest family in the area. By the middle of the century, all the wealthy families had built their own towers bringing the total to seventy-two towers. A law was established in 1255 that no towers could be built that were higher than the Torre Rognosa. This ended a rivalry between two families called the Ardinghellis and the Salvuccis.

Jaq read it again and again before telling Atalia all about the envelope he had delivered to Mr. Dino in which he also had the surname Salvucci. Was there a link?

Jaq and Atalia chatted for ages until Greta appeared at the door and reminded Jaq that he ought to get to bed and catch-up on some sleep before school the next day.

Atalia waited until Greta had gone to bed before slipping outside into the back garden. Jaq could hear Atalia going downstairs but decided that the mystery of Mr. Dino's surname (and possible ancestry) was more interesting than what Atalia was doing outside.

*

It was the next evening that Jaq decided that he would try another visit to Dino's house, only this time he wanted to know for certain that Dino was not there. He waited long and hard until Dino eventually left the house and started walking in the direction of the towers. Jaq went and knocked on the front door of the house. The same woman appeared at the door.

'You again,' she said. 'What do you want, Jaq?'

'Is Mr. Dino in?' Jaq asked innocently.

'No, he's just gone out,' replied the woman.

'Not a problem, perhaps I'll try again tomorrow,' said Jaq. 'Thank you Mrs. Salvucci.'

'That's quite alright, Jaq. Thank you.'

Aah, thought Jaq, so she didn't have a problem with the name Salvucci either. In Jaq's mind the mystery was now solved – Dino's surname was Salvucci. But that left three more unsolved mysteries:

1. Why did Dino use the name 'Du Lupe'?

2. Was Dino really related to Franco Du Lupe at all?

3. What was the ancestral connection between Dino and the builders of the towers in the 13th Century?

He hoped Atalia might know some of the answers.

Chapter 10

'Aaagh! Girls!' exclaimed Marco in the playground at school one day. 'Why do they have to be so giggly and chattery about everything?'

'Don't ask me,' said Jaq. 'I'm just glad I'm not one of them. Look at the way they are all crowding around each other over there. Anyone would think a celebrity was about to arrive or something.'

He pointed to where a group of girls, all in his year group, were whispering, sniggering and then letting out roars of laughter.

'What's it all about, then?' asked Marco, still curious that he may be missing out on some important gossip or occasion.

'It's about Alina Tonella's birthday party,' replied Jaq. 'It's happening next weekend and all the girls are invited. Apparently, it's going to be some big banquet at her father's hotel at the bottom of town. It sounds totally boring to me.'

'Hmm, I agree,' snorted Marco. The interest in the activity now ceasing in his mind as it bore no reference to sport.

The school bell rang and they all filed into class, the girls still chattering and the boys looking suitably unimpressed. Jaq wasn't quite sure what was worse –

a double Maths lesson or listening to the ongoing whispers and giggles of the girls sat around him.

*

Alina Tonella had wanted a particularly special party. With her father now owning the best hotel in San Gimignano, she wanted to make her birthday the news of the town. The party, as Jaq had said, was to be held in the restaurant of the hotel. There would be a special five-course meal with non-alcoholic cocktails (otherwise known as 'mocktails') served alongside. Every girl in the year group had been invited as well as a few mothers to help with waitressing and various other roles.

There would be live music, mainly classical or operatic as well as some disco music after the meal for dancing. The restaurant would be decorated up with hundreds of bouquets of flowers plus balloons, ribbons and much more. It was almost as if it was going to be a fairy-tale wedding celebration instead of a birthday party – but everyone knew that the Tonellas had no shortage of money and would 'splash out' on the occasion.

Not only this, but Alina had requested for all the girls to come to the hotel in advance of the meal to have a massage, their hair styled, make-up professionally applied, and their nails manicured, so that they would look their absolute best for the birthday meal.

The meal would consist of a starter, a two-course traditional Italian dinner, a dessert and a coffee. This would be followed by further refreshments later on in the evening.

Naturally the whole town was talking about it as most people had at least one daughter or niece who would be attending the party. As more and more neighbours and associates offered their own suggestions and ideas, so the whole concept of the party was growing to ridiculous proportions. Mr. Tonella had to eventually thank everyone for their input but explain that he felt that Alina shouldn't have special preference over the other girls in the town. This was a little 'tongue-in-cheek' as he himself knew that no-one else in the town could match the same standard of party as that of his own daughter Alina's. Perhaps, he suggested, that whilst this was Alina's birthday, the girls could consider it one big party for all of them.

No presents were expected from Alina's friends. In this way, Alina had a good heart and, instead, wanted a charity collection to help orphans in the Middle East. This, she felt, was a worthwhile cause. She would, of course, send the orphans a photo of her and her friends on her birthday so that they could see who the money was coming from. Not such a good idea of course.

*

Greta was relieved to not be involved at all. Atalia was not in Alina's year group. Also, as it was a girl's only party, it meant Jaq would not be invited either.

'It's a good thing you two aren't still together,' mumbled Greta to Jaq one evening. 'Look at all the fuss there would have been if you had had to go to the party.'

'You wouldn't get me dressed up looking like a penguin,' snorted Jaq. 'I would have gone in my t-shirt and jeans.'

'You wouldn't have even got in the door wearing that,' laughed Atalia. 'I think you're very wise to not be seeing Alina anymore.'

Jaq pondered over the idea and agreed that he was fortunate to not be involved with this ridiculous party. It had been quite a while since he and Alina had broken up and he certainly had no interest in developing any further relationships now.

*

Two days later however the situation had to be re-examined. Two letters arrived in the post. The first was an invitation inviting Greta to help at the party by cooking some of her Mediterranean bread for the first course of the meal. Greta naturally wanted to refuse but also realised the negative impact this would have upon her standing and reputation in the community. The last thing she would want would be to be seen as unsociable. Greta picked up the phone and called Mr. Tonella and explained that she would be only too happy to help.

The second letter was an invitation for Atalia to come to the party as Alina's special guest. Atalia was simply shocked.

'I'm not sure that I want to go,' said Atalia. 'I don't really know Alina – and besides I will be the only girl there who isn't in her year group at school. None of the other girls will know who I am. Alina will have all her friends there – she doesn't need me.'

Atalia knew that her reasons didn't overly sound convincing, but she also felt uncomfortable to have been invited. Her mind started to ask questions and she quickly withdrew herself to her bedroom to meditate on the invitation.

*

It was the next morning that Atalia announced to both Greta and Jaq that she would go to the party on certain conditions. The first being that she didn't attend before the meal started. Being dressed up as a princess was not Atalia's style. Second, that she kept a fairly low profile throughout the evening. She figured that with Greta being in the kitchen, she could always get back-up support if she needed it – and that they both might be able to leave the party early if needs be.

Greta agreed that this was probably the best solution and would not cause any offence to anyone.

'I think she has invited me for your sake,' Atalia told Greta. 'It would be a little embarrassing for you to be helping without me being there when everyone in the town knows that I am living here.'

Jaq nodded. It made some sense he supposed. He, of course, would have an evening at home to himself – a very rare occurrence in his house and so he would invite Marco to come around for a boy's night in – some food and a movie perhaps.

*

On the night of the party, the hotel was looking magnificent. The marble steps up to the hotel entrance had all been polished and a red carpet laid out, much like they do at the Oscars. The glass doors were gleaming, and the gold lettering welcomed everyone to 'Tonellas'.

Inside, the frescoed walls told of great Italian history, art and architecture. There were painted scenes from the baroque era in the seventeenth century in whites, greens, golds, blues and reds. There were great images of angels blowing trumpets, clouds of glory and great heroes of strength, might and faith.

Inside the restaurant, the circular banqueting tables were decorated with white and blue cloths, covered with sequins and stars. The cutlery shone with the reflection of the chandeliers overhead. The cocktail glasses shimmering, and the flowers ornately arranged in every direction that you could look.

The fifteen musicians were seated at the far end on a small constructed stage within an alcove area. Their brass, stringed and wind instruments being played beautifully with such great skill and emotion that the atmosphere was almost enchanting.

All around stood many, many girls dressed in fine clothes, beautiful headpieces, expensive shoes and beautifully made up with jewellery and accessories in their hair, on their fingers and around their necks.

Atalia felt underdressed in her pale lemon dress with a short sleeved white cardigan over the top and a small hair clip to the right-hand side of her hair. She wore no make-up and was quite content to be herself. This didn't change the fact however that in comparison to all the other girls, she looked as if she had only just arrived – which in all respects was true.

'Can we go home now?' she whispered to Greta.

'No, we can't' replied Greta. 'Don't worry, you'll be fine. I'll be in the serving area if you need me.'

Atalia ignored the other girls who were all grouped up, chatting, laughing and comparing themselves to one another. At least the fact that no-one knew who she was would be a relief and, in that respect, she would probably be left alone.

A bell sounded and Mrs. Tonella announced that it was time for everyone to take their places at the tables. Atalia carefully looked around for the place which had her name card on it. This was going to be difficult anyway, she told herself. 'I am going to end up sat around with a whole group of girls who won't know who I am and will want to ask questions that I don't want to answer.' She continued looking around for her name but couldn't see it. In the distance, Mr. and Mrs. Tonella were sitting down at the head-table with Alina next to them surrounded by family relatives including uncles, aunts and cousins – no boys of course.

Atalia had a sudden moment of panic. *What happened if there wasn't a seat for her? How embarrassing would that be? She would be exposed in front of everyone for being there – the mistaken guest, the unknown person, the misfit…*

'Stop it!' she told herself. She paused and stood still for a moment as if listening for divine inspiration. 'Yes, I am supposed to be here,' she continued. 'I have an invitation in my pocket.' She pulled it out and read it to make sure.

A hand rested on her back. 'Atalia,' started Mrs. Tonella who had appeared from behind her. 'You're over here,' pointing in the direction of the head-table. 'Alina's put a special place right next to her for you.'

Atalia's mind froze for a moment. *The head-table?! Next to Alina?! On one hand, what a privilege. On the other hand, what on earth was going on?* She paused for a moment and then the answer came to her. *She wants something,* Atalia thought. *I don't know what it is, but she wants something.*

*

None of the other girls made any comment about Atalia being sat next to Alina. They supposedly assumed that she was related in some way. Atalia was determined to make sure that they didn't find out otherwise.

She didn't have to wait long before she found out why Alina had invited her.

'I want to ask you a favour,' Alina whispered to her over the second main course.

'What would that be?' asked Atalia, quite intrigued by now that she herself was experiencing this great birthday celebration in style all for the sake of a favour.

'Your brother, Jaq…' Alina started.

'What about him?'

'Well… I really miss him, and I want us to get back together again, but I don't know how,' continued Alina.

'Jaq's not particularly interested in girls at the moment,' replied Atalia. 'But I can mention something to him if you want.'

'That would be great,' whispered Alina, 'and give him this as well, would you?' She pulled out an envelope with Jaq's name on it.

'Of course,' replied Atalia taking the envelope. 'What's in it?'

'Just a little something,' replied Alina, blushing slightly. '

Atalia put the envelope in her pocket and continued eating, smiling to herself. *The only reason she had been invited to this party was for Alina to ask for a matchmaking favour.*

'Oh, by the way,' Alina continued. 'I am going to have to spend the rest of the evening talking to my friends. You can chat to my parents and cousins if you like. But please stay until the end. I need to ask you something when everyone has gone. I'll arrange for my father to drop you home.'

With that, Alina whispered to her mother and subsequently left the head-table. Atalia didn't see Alina again for the rest of the birthday party.

*

'How was the party?' retorted Jaq scornfully the next morning.

'It was good,' replied Atalia modestly.

'You girls certainly ate enough to put the town out of food for the next month,' said Greta. 'I had never seen so much food at the start and so few left-overs at the end.'

'Jaq… Alina gave me an envelope to give to you.'

Strange, thought Jaq. He took the envelope from Atalia's hand and ripped it open. It had a note inside that said, 'Really missing you. Hope you enjoy this gift.' With it was a ticket to the baseball finals in Rome.

'The baseball finals, wow!' replied Jaq, but his excitement quickly changed into solemnity. 'No! If Alina thinks that this means we are going to be friends again, she has another thing coming. I don't want to get caught up into all that namby-pamby, poshy, dressy-up stuff like that party last night. I don't want to be her friend.'

'I think she's quite sincere,' replied Atalia. 'She likes you, Jaq.'

'No,' said Jaq. 'Next time I see her, I will tell her.' He marched out the room as if someone had just delivered a military assignment.

'Oh well,' said Atalia. 'I guess Alina will get over it.'

'I am sure she will,' replied Greta. 'At least you managed to enjoy a party out of it, Atalia.'

'Yes…' said Atalia thoughtfully. 'There's also something else…'

'Oh yes?' enquired Greta.

'Yes. Alina told me just before I came home last night that there were some secret caves underneath the hotel. She wants me to come and see them.'

'You be careful,' warned Greta.

'Oh, it's no worry,' said Atalia. 'They're all illuminated by electric lights. Alina is intrigued to know all about them and thought I might be able to help.'

'I'm sure with all your knowledge, you probably can,' smiled Greta. 'When are you going?'

'Next Wednesday night,' answered Atalia. 'Who knows what we shall find?'

Chapter 11

Jaq had spent much time researching the address for Franco Du Lupe on his computer. He was convinced that if he wanted to confront Dino with the truth about his identity and his surname that he needed more evidence. Aside from which, what was Dino achieving by deceiving everyone into thinking his name was different even to the point of advertising it on the staff notice board.

Eventually, Jaq found the address of the old philosopher. It was apparent that Mr. Franco Du Lupe now lived in Trieste, a town in the north east of the country. Jaq immediately started penning a letter to him asking whether he was aware of a philosophy teacher called Dino who was apparently claiming to be his son, and was this the truth or wasn't it? Had he heard of the name Dino Salvucci and did that have any significance? On finishing the letter, he showed it to Atalia who gave Jaq a most disapproving stare that he knew almost immediately that he would need her help to draft something a little more diplomatic.

Atalia suggested that maybe some comments that buttered Mr. Du Lupe up to start with might be more favourably viewed upon.

'How about telling him how much you enjoy studying philosophy and that you admire his ideas and thinking?'

'But I don't,' replied Jaq indignantly.

'Yes, you know that, and I know that – but he doesn't, does he? If he thinks that you respect him, he is probably going to be more willing to respond to you and answer some of your questions.'

'I guess so. Am I wasting my time, Atalia?'

'On one hand, maybe. On the other hand, you will only be satisfied when you know the answers, so let's just get this letter done, shall we?'

Jaq picked up the pen again whilst Atalia dictated the words and phrases that he should use:

Dear Mr. Franco Du Lupe,

My name is Jaq Alfonsi and I am a secondary school philosophy student in San Gimignano. I thoroughly enjoy learning this subject and am fascinated by your own thinking and ideas.

My teacher, Mr. Dino Salvucci, admires you so much that he often calls himself Mr. Dino Du Lupe. He hasn't yet told us whether the two of you are indeed related – but like you, he has an incredible mind and I am getting excellent grades in his class.

(Jaq had to admit however that his excellent grades had more to do with the help he was receiving from Atalia than Dino's teaching.)

I was wondering whether you would have any additional reading or resources you could recommend helping me advance my understanding further.

It would be great to become a great philosopher like you one day.

With thanks,

Jaq Alfonsi.

He and Atalia read the letter over and over again before finally putting it in an envelope and posting it to Trieste, enclosing a self-addressed envelope to try and guarantee a reply.

'I know what he will say when he gets it,' said Atalia to Jaq as they walked back from the post box.

'Something like… I don't know what you are talking about. Please leave me alone,' suggested Jaq.

'No, I don't think so,' replied Atalia in a very matter of fact tone. 'He is going to write something like: Dear Jaq, thank you for your kind letter. I am glad you enjoy learning philosophy. I haven't heard of your teacher Dino Salvucci, but I am honoured by the fact that he wants to name himself after me.'

'And then,' Atalia continued, 'he will write and recommend some books that you should study to help you progress further with philosophy.'

'Hmm…' replied Jaq retortingly, 'we shall see, won't we?'

The reply came within a day or two. The handwriting was very scrawny and somehow the old philosopher had found the time to write at least two or three pages of information, much of which Jaq didn't have a clue about. The main points of interest for him was the opening paragraph of the letter and the information about Dino. It read:

Dear Jaq,

Thank you for your kind letter. I am glad you enjoy learning philosophy. There is always so much to consider and rationalise about the world around you...

Hang on a minute, thought Jaq. He cast his mind back to the conversation he and Atalia had had when they walked back from the post-box – *those introductory lines were exactly the same as Atalia had said that he would say!* He read it again.

Dear Jaq,

Thank you for your kind letter. I am glad you enjoy learning philosophy...

That was exactly what she had said. This had Jaq's mind wondering. *Did Atalia have some connection herself with Franco Du Lupe? Maybe she knew him personally. Or was Atalia just psychic – much like the day when his mother fell off the balcony?*

He decided to leave these thoughts on hold. For the moment he wanted to find out the truth about Dino. He scrolled through the next page and a half before he found the paragraph he was looking for.

I am flattered by the fact that your teacher is calling himself after me. He must think I am an amazing philosopher, although I see myself just as an ordinary man with some extraordinary ideas. As for knowing your teacher, I don't believe I have ever met a person called Dino Salvucci. He certainly is of no relation to me as I have neither siblings nor children of my own…

So, the whole Franco Du Lupe thing about being Dino's father was a complete farce. Dino had made up the whole scenario, thought Jaq. *But why? For certain his philosophy teacher's actual name was Dino Salvucci.*

Jaq wondered whether he ought to go and present these findings to the headteacher along with the letter from Franco Du Lupe. He could also invite Mrs. Salvucci to come along to the meeting as well who would then testify that her husband was indeed Dino Salvucci and not Du Lupe.

Jaq re-enacted the whole scenario in his mind. *The headteacher would expose Dino for being a fake and then sack him. He would then reward Jaq handsomely for being such a clever student and give him honorary grades for his exams, which he then wouldn't have to sit.* It seemed great.

His mind came back to reality when Greta walked in and asked him whether he had completed his homework yet and, if not, why not?

'Sorry, mama. My mind was somewhere else.'

'Well, get it back on course, Jaq. That mathematics homework is not going to do itself now, is it?'

Jaq grunted. *His mother was right. He would need to wait and think a bit harder about what he would do about Dino.*

*

It was about 1am in the morning when Atalia knocked on Jaq's bedroom. There was no response so Atalia crept in and shook him gently to wake him.

'Jaq…Jaq…'

Jaq stirred with a start. 'What?…What are you doing in here?'

'I know who the Salvuccis are.'

'You do?' said Jaq, waking up a lot more quickly.

'Well, I know who they were.'

'When did you find this out?'

'About twenty minutes ago. I thought you would want to know straight away.'

'But it's the middle of the night, Atalia.'

Jaq switched his bedside lamp on and sat himself up in bed, rubbing his eyes and trying to concentrate on what Atalia was telling him. He still wasn't quite sure at this point why it couldn't have waited until the morning.

'You know that you said you saw Dino up at the towers?' started Atalia.

'Yes,' replied Jaq, intrigued.

'Well, his family ancestry is all linked to two of the towers.'

'What?!' replied Jaq. 'Tell me more…'

'The Salvucci family were known as Ghibellines and they were rivals with the Guelphs.'

'You're losing me already,' said Jaq.

'Just listen!' hissed Atalia. 'There was a law passed in the 13th Century that forbid anyone to build a tower that was more than fifty-two metres high.'

'But some of the towers are much higher than fifty-two metres,' exclaimed Jaq.

'Exactly!' said Atalia. 'The Salvucci family then broke the law and built two towers higher than the permitted height.'

'I think I see what you're getting at, Atalia,' said Jaq. 'You think that Dino has some interest in the towers because of his ancestry?'

'Precisely!' Atalia smiled.

'That's brilliant,' said Jaq, 'and so Dino is using the name Du Lupe so that no-one knows that he really is part of the Salvucci family.'

'Yes.'

'The only thing is,' said Jaq. 'Why didn't Mrs. Salvucci react when I called her by her real surname?'

'Perhaps she just wasn't thinking,' said Atalia.

Jaq pondered. *He really did have a lot of information to confront Dino with now. First, the response from Mrs.*

Salvucci; second, the letter from Franco Du Lupe; and thirdly, the information from Atalia. The confrontation was going to be most interesting.

*

Jaq decided that he would not involve the headteacher. *Better to take things into his own hands*, he concluded. He waited behind at the end of the lesson and asked if he and Marco could talk to Dino during the lunch break. Jaq was aware that Marco would have no idea about what he would be talking about, but at least he would be there for back-up if needed.

*

'I don't believe it,' declared Dino. 'What made you look up all this information and write these letters and everything?'

'Marco and I saw you up at the towers, didn't we, Marco?'

Marco nodded in agreement.

'And,' Jaq continued. 'there's the confusion between why your name is Du Lupe on the staff board but is actually Salvucci in real life.'

'Jaq, listen,' started Dino. 'I am sure you are thinking that this is all quite suspicious and it really isn't. My real surname is Salvucci and my ancestry is connected to two of the towers here in the town. That is why I am so fascinated by the architecture and wanting to know more. The only time I can get to look at the towers properly without being disturbed is at night which is why I go.'

'But why did you say that your father was Franco Du Lupe?'

'When I trained to be a philosophy teacher I found out about the work of Franco Du Lupe and respected his ideas a lot. He became my hero, my idol if you like.'

'But why use his name?' enquired Jaq.

'I didn't want people at San Gimignano knowing that my surname was Salvucci. My ancestors had some serious fallouts with others in the town over the towers and whilst that was years ago, there are people who know their history really well and I didn't want any confrontation over my family history.'

Dino looked at the miserable expression on Jaq's face.

'I am sorry if I have disappointed you with the truth,' Dino said. 'I am sure you were convinced that there was a big drama in it all, but there's not.'

'That's okay. Thank you, Mr. Du Lupe.'

'You got it,' replied Dino. 'This is our secret, okay?'

'Okay,' said Jaq. Marco nodded in agreement.

'By the way,' said Dino, just as Jaq and Marco were about to go out the door. 'How did you find out all that information about the Salvuccis? The history records are quite hard to get hold of, you know.'

'My sister told me,' said Jaq, innocently.

'Aah, yes, your intriguing sister who seems to know everything...' said Dino. 'I must meet her sometime.'

*

'What an anti-climax!' said Jaq.

'I didn't understand all of it,' said Marco, 'but I'll tell you one thing. I don't believe him!'

'You don't?' Jaq looked surprised.

'No.'

'Why?'

'Because it doesn't explain why he still insists on going to the towers every night. Also, it doesn't explain why the town called Dino's wife, Mrs. Salvucci. Surely the town are clever enough to put two and two together to make four and work out that Dino's name must be Salvucci.'

Jaq stood at stared at Marco in amazement. *Perhaps he's not so ignorant after all, he thought.*

'Marco, you may be right,' he said at last. 'I shall have to talk to Atalia. Perhaps she will know.'

Chapter 12

Jaq quickly made up his mind that he wouldn't ask Atalia after all. Whilst he knew that she was smart, clever and always willing to help, he felt that it was time that he came into his own and found out some information for himself. He would, of course, rely on a little help from Marco though.

Arrangements were quickly established that they would monitor the activity of Dino at the tower. Marco would have a camera and take photos of the areas in and around the tower that Dino showed particular interest in. Once Dino had departed, Marco would then take close up shots of the same spots. In this way, the two boys would then be able to look at the photos on the laptop back at home and see if they could notice any particular features that would help solve the clues behind what Dino was really up to at the towers.

In the meantime, Jaq would have a clipboard and pencil. He would be making notes of anything that Dino did, the timings of the visits, the observations made and, of course, the evidence from Marco's photographs. He would also keep an ongoing record chart for each visit so that comparisons could be made as and when were necessary. He didn't quite know yet what those comparisons would be, so assured Marco that everything was bound to become clear given a certain amount of time and evidence.

Jaq thought through the plan again. *Was there anything that he and Marco had missed? They would need to find some reason for meeting up every evening so that neither family or parent became suspicious as to what the boys were up to.*

Marco suggested that a basketball match could be coming up soon and therefore they were going to practise every evening. Jaq could understand Marco's thinking, but realised that when there were no further details about the tournament to parents, they would then know they were lying.

'Telling lies can be like a snowball rolling down a hill,' Jaq informed Marco. 'You tell one small one, and then you end up telling another one to cover the first one, and then another one to cover up the second one and so on, until you end up with one big snowball of lies that goes out of control.'

Marco thought long and hard about this concept. *Jaq was probably right – he normally was. They would need a better excuse then.*

'Why don't we tell our families that we have been set a nature project based around the towers? They know that we have been looking at the architecture of San Gimignano, and they know that we have a teacher who is very interested in the towers. We could say that we are having to observe what creatures appear at the towers at night and record it down.'

'That's an excellent idea,' replied Marco. 'No-one would think of questioning us. The project could last about two to three weeks.'

'That should give us enough time to work out what Dino is up to,' said Jaq.

Both boys looked at each other as if a stroke of genius had just hit them. They laughed excitedly and jumped to their feet.

'Right, when shall we start?'

'Tonight, of course,' Jaq replied. 'The sooner we start the better.'

*

Neither Greta nor Atalia were surprised when Jaq said about the nature project. Jaq had been expecting lots of questions about what creatures they were going to be looking for, and so he had prepared some good answers; but all had proved unnecessary. *Interesting,* thought Jaq, *that Atalia is clearly not interested in animals as he had previously wondered whether Atalia might have asked to come with him to help with the nature project, which could have been a little difficult to explain why she couldn't.* He was therefore quite relieved that this hadn't happened.

Up in his bedroom, Jaq prepared his rucksack with everything that he needed. First, he put in the clipboard, paper and pencil – with one extra pencil in case he needed it. Next, went in his little mini torch – as it could be dark by the time Dino left, he might need these to see what he would be writing on the clipboard. Next, went in his mackintosh (raincoat) so that if the weather did become inclement, he would not get caught out. Next, the camera was put in the bag. Whilst Marco was going to use his own camera, Jaq thought that an extra one might come in useful. He carefully made sure that the flash had been turned off. He certainly wouldn't want to give the game away. Finally, Jaq popped into the kitchen and made himself a flask of hot chocolate.

'It will keep me warm whilst I am waiting for nature,' he told Greta, who nodded approvingly.

'Don't forget your hat,' said Greta. 'I don't want your head getting cold.'

True, thought Jaq. *The last thing he would want would be a cold. That would stop everything.* He went and got the hat and put it on his head.

'What time will you be home?' asked Greta.

'I don't know, Mama. It depends on how long Dino is up there…' He stopped, realising what he had said.

'Oh, Dino's up there with you as well, is he?' asked Greta. 'The poor man is working overtime. I hope they're paying him to work with you boys each night.'

'Well, he's just there tonight to get us started,' bluffed Jaq. 'Help us to look in the right places.'

'Good idea,' replied Greta.

Jaq breathed a sigh of relief. The bluff had worked, and he wouldn't get found out. He quickly grabbed his things and ran out the front door, closing it behind him.

'I've never seen Jaq so enthusiastic to do his homework,' Greta told Atalia. 'Maybe nature spotting has really captured his imagination.'

'I guess it has,' replied Atalia. 'I saw him and Marco having a long chat about it the other day. I couldn't hear what exactly they were saying, but I know it was about being up at the towers for the next few nights to watch what activity was happening there.'

'Well, don't be surprised if he loses enthusiasm after a week,' said Greta. 'It's not unusual for Jaq to be good at starting something and not so good at finishing it.'

Atalia smiled. She knew Jaq well enough now to know that Greta was telling the absolute truth.

*

Outside, Marco had been waiting for Jaq from the opposite side of the street. He too had his rucksack fully packed and ready to go. Both boys walked silently and almost in unison together towards the Devil's Tower where they would wait to see what Dino would get up to. It felt kind of like a military operation of some sort – as if they were going to set up base and monitor the activities of the enemy – not that Dino was an enemy of course.

They found themselves a convenient viewing point from behind a bush, looking out onto the entrance of the Devil's Tower. From here, they would see Dino arrive. If necessary, they could then change their position once Dino was settled on one particular spot.

The dark, evening clouds moved in and slowly the sky turned black. A light shower of rain descended and both boys quickly put the hoods on their raincoats up. Marco got out his binoculars and started looking for any sign of Dino on his way. Jaq squatted, gazing into the distance. He was slightly frustrated that he couldn't get his clipboard and paper out because of the weather so resorted to having a drink of his hot chocolate instead.

'Look,' hissed Marco. 'Here he comes now.'

The figure of a man wearing a long black coat came walking towards the towers. He stopped, looked around and then drew near to the entrance way of the Devil's Tower. From his pocket, a camera appeared, and the man took a couple of shots. The flash bounced off the tower's stones.

'He's taking photos,' exclaimed Jaq. 'What does he want those for?'

'Don't ask me,' said Marco. 'Look! What's he doing now?'

The figure had bent down outside the entrance way and appeared to be stroking the ground around the outside of the tower. First, stroking, then knocking.

This is really strange, thought Jaq. *Normally, Dino spends most of his time inside the tower; but tonight, he was concentrating on the area around the outside. Whatever he was doing had to be important. No-one in their right mind would normally go hunting around the outside of the tower in the rain.*

Suddenly, there was a noise that made Jaq jump. Marco sneezed. Some people have sneezes which are quiet or barely noticeable. By contrast, Marco had a sneeze which was fast, sudden and could wake an entire neighbourhood.

'Who's there?' came the voice of the figure.

Jaq quickly put his hands to his mouth and made a hooting sound, resembling that of an owl or some other bird of prey.

'What are you doing?' hissed Marco.

'Trying to cover up your sneeze with an owl hoot,' said Jaq, 'before Dino discovers that we are watching him.'

'An owl hoot?' whispered Marco. 'You call that an owl hoot? It was more like an Frecciarossa 1000 train coming through.'

'Oh yes? Well, your sneeze sounded more like an Alitalia airbus coming into land,' hissed Jaq. 'You could have given us away.'

'I still might have done,' replied Marco. 'The man is walking this direction.'

'Quick, let's make a run for it,' said Jaq. 'We could just get away in time.'

'No,' replied Marco. 'If we run, he'll know we have been here. If we stay, then we might not get discovered at all.'

Jaq looked at Marco uncertainly. The figure was still walking in their direction. His mind started working through the forthcoming dialogue that he would have to give to Dino, explaining why he and Marco were there – and why they hadn't believed him after their last conversation.

But Jaq didn't need to fear. The figure stopped, listened for a moment and then turned around to return to the place where he had been looking at the ground.

Jaq could feel his heart pumping wildly in his chest, but now, he could breathe again, and he gave out a long, silent sigh of relief. Marco picked up the binoculars again and started to observe more of what was going on.

Suddenly, Marco jerked on Jaq's arm. 'Jaq! Look! Someone else is coming!'

'What?!' exclaimed Jaq. He looked through Marco's binoculars. The second person was also a man wearing a black coat. He was taller and slimmer than the first man and walked with a much quicker pace. Jaq continued to watch as the man arrived at the towers, but seemingly not expecting anyone else to be there. The more Jaq stared at the second man, the more he became convinced that the second man was, in fact, Dino. This left the terrible question of who the first man was. *Maybe Dino had an accomplice or something* – but then it didn't appear that either of the two men had expected the other to be present.

Indeed, they hadn't, for all of a sudden, the second man spotted the first man and shouted something to him. Jaq strained his ears to try and hear what the man was saying, but the hood on his raincoat was muffling the sound. He wondered about dropping the hood down but decided that it was too wet for that.

Both boys continued to watch as the first man responded and started shouting back at the second man. The two men had walked towards each other. The first was waving his arms about all over the place. Jaq noticed how tubby this first man looked and how it couldn't be Dino at all. Dino had to be the second man.

The second man was doing a lot of pointing at the first man, shouting something, and putting up his fists. The first man laughed and started putting up his fists too.

'There's going to be a fight,' said Marco. 'I wonder who will win.'

'I just wonder who the first man is,' replied Jaq.

They watched as the first man made an attempted swing at the second man. It winded him but not enough to stop a retaliation. The second man pushed the first man's chest and then kicked him hard. The first man shouted back something and then the fight got into full flow. There were punches, ducking and diving, pushes, headlocks, elbow jabs until eventually the first man fell onto the floor. The second man walked over, laughed and said something, before walking off, back in the direction of the town, wiping his brow and cleaning himself off as he went.

Jaq and Marco looked at each other. The last thing they had been expecting to see was two grown men fighting.

Out of nowhere came an owl hoot.

'Shut up, Marco,' said Jaq. 'We don't need you being stupid right now.'

'It's not me,' said Marco. 'Look, there's an owl just landed on the ledge of the tower over there.'

'Who cares?' retorted Jaq.

'Err… we're supposed to be here on a nature watch. At least if we get it down on paper, we have something to show someone if they ask how we got on.'

'Okay, fair point,' groaned Jaq, 'but I am more interested to know who that man on the ground is.'

Marco kept an eye whilst Jaq wrote down about the owl on his clipboard.

'He's not moving, Jaq. I wonder if he's dead,' queried Marco.

'I doubt he's dead,' replied Jaq.

'Well, he might be badly hurt or even unconscious,' said Marco.

Jaq turned and looked at Marco sternly. 'Look,' he started. 'No-one knows we're here. We're not involved. If we hadn't come here tonight, that man over there would be lying on the ground until someone found him.'

'But you're wrong,' replied Marco with a strong sense of indignation. 'For once, Jaq, I know what I'm talking about. People do know that we're here. We've both told our families that we're up here doing a nature observation. Now if that man over there proves to be dead, then someone is going to be coming around to talk to us about whether we saw anything. And…,' Marco continued, building his case for the prosecution quite convincingly, 'and, if they do find out we were here, then they are going to ask us, what we were doing. Our cover will be blown, and goodness knows what trouble we could find ourselves in.'

Jaq thought long and hard. *They were in a no-win situation. Either way, someone would know that they were there.*

'Okay…' retreated Jaq. 'Let's go and see if our mystery man is dead.'

They gathered up their belongings and walked over to the figure who was still lying face down on the ground but making groaning noises.

'He is still alive,' said Jaq. 'Help me turn him over, Marco.'

Together they heaved the short, but heavy body over. The man was definitely breathing alright.

'Are you alright?' asked Marco, loudly.

'Get… me… home…' puffed the man, slowly with the little energy he had left.

'Marco, put your torch on – let's see whether we recognise this person.'

Marco got out his torch and shot it in the man's face. When he did, both boys got quite a shock.

'It's Mr. Tonella!' said Jaq. 'What are you doing here?'

*

Chapter 13

Within a few days, Mr. Tonella was feeling fully recovered, but maintaining a resentment to his new-found enemy called Dino. When asked about the incident, he was reluctant to give any details, other than the fact that they had had a disagreement and that he was right, and Dino was wrong.

Dino likewise had some signs of bruising, Jaq noticed, but nothing that anyone would particular notice if they hadn't witnessed the fight themselves. Marco and Jaq decided that it was probably best to not mention their presence being there; but it was too late. Mr. Tonella had already informed the whole neighbourhood of the kindness of the two boys who had come to his rescue on that particular evening.

No-one had queried or mentioned about the presence of the two boys at the towers that night, and both families still presumed that it was for the nature project. The reputation of Dino however was being frowned upon: How did a teacher in charge of a nature trip end up in a confrontational fight? The gossip channels would soon start around the town but would finish as quickly as they started.

'It's like having pizza for dinner,' Greta once said. 'No sooner does it arrive than it's gone.'

Mr. Tonella had personally sent Jaq and Marco gifts of tickets to a basketball match – both boys were tremendously excited and grateful for the generosity they had been shown. The gifts themselves had been delivered by Alina who was now in great adoration of Jaq and made it very clear how heroic she considered him to be and how 'every princess needs a handsome knight to protect her.'

Jaq was not foolish in recognising that Alina was trying to flatter him and regain his friendship. On one hand, he was reluctant to do so, particularly when he reflected back on Alina's extravagant birthday party; on the other hand, however, it would be nice to have someone who really admired him particularly if she delivered more gifts, even if they were ultimately from her father. He eventually relented and the two were chatting away together, hand in hand, as if they had never broken up.

In light of all of this, Atalia wondered whether the invitation back to the hotel the following night was still open. The idea of the secret caves had sounded quite exciting, but as Alina had invited her on the night of her birthday in an attempt to win Jaq back, she didn't know if the offer still stood.

'You are still coming tomorrow night, aren't you?' asked Alina with a playful look in her eye.

'I didn't know if you still wanted me to,' said Atalia. 'I won't be offended if you don't, now that you and Jaq are back together.'

'Of course, I want you to come,' said Alina. 'There is a great mystery to be worked out at the hotel and I think you are just the person to solve it. It will be very exciting to find things out together.'

Atalia smiled back. 'Will Jaq be coming as well?' she asked.

'No,' Alina chuckled. 'It's for us, girls, to solve this one. Besides I will probably see Jaq quite a lot during the day tomorrow, so it will be good to chat together in the evening.'

Jaq raised his eyebrows and looked embarrassed. He desperately hoped that Alina's new friendship with Atalia wasn't going to be a tell-tale one all about him.

'I'm not like that, Jaq,' Atalia protested. 'You should know that by now!'

'I know,' said Jaq. 'It's just I hate the way girls have to gossip about us, boys. We never do the same about girls.'

'I should hope not,' said Atalia, walking out of the living room and up to her bedroom for a little peace and quiet for a while.

*

Atalia didn't see Jaq until dinner time the next day. He had left just before breakfast and spent the day, presumably, with Alina.

Straight after dinner however, Atalia got herself ready in some black trousers, a white top and a black cardigan with some black trainers on for comfortability. She wanted to go looking fairly smart, as the hotel was particularly expensive, but at the same time, be dressed practically for seeing the caves – whatever that entailed.

*

Alina was waiting in the hotel foyer for her. She gave her a hug on arrival and quickly escorted her along some of the back passages of the hotel until they reached an old doorway.

'Are you ready for this?' asked Alina excitedly. 'You are going to love it!'

She unlocked the old wooden door and slowly pulled it towards her. It made a loud creaking noise as the wood moved on the old hinges. Atalia strained her eyes to try and see what was there, but all she could see was darkness. Then Alina flicked a switch just inside the door and a whole tunnel was illuminated. The brown rocky walls on either side of the tunnel clearly dated back many years. They looked mottled, dirty, aged and solid. It was obvious that when this tunnel was built, it had been made by skilled workmen who were ensuring the safety and well-being of themselves as well as the people who would be going through them in the future. *Considering they would have built these by candlelight*, Atalia thought, *they would have been working under quite harsh conditions.*

The tunnel itself was about four-foot-wide and about fifty foot long.

'Come on,' said Alina. 'This is nothing. Come and see what's further down.'

She stepped into the tunnel with Atalia close behind her, leaving the old wooden door ajar behind her, ensuring that she still had the keys in her hand.

'All this lighting looks quite modern,' said Atalia.

'It is,' replied Alina. 'My father installed it so that we could go down into these caves and explore them further without any fear or danger.'

'What a relief!' exclaimed Atalia.

Together they walked down to the end of the tunnel, turned right and along a similar tunnel of about the same length. Off to the left and the right were more smaller tunnels. It appeared that this was like a subterranean world with many different ways you could go.

'You would get so easily lost down here,' said Atalia.

'I know,' said Alina excitedly. 'That's another reason why father put the lights in. Providing we stay on the tunnels with the lights on, we know that we won't get lost.'

'So, what's your father going to do with this lot?' asked Atalia.

'Well, I guess, one day, we will be able to do tours for the hotel guests down here, but it's not all finished yet Atalia. We still have more to do.'

'Your father must spend a lot of time down here then?' questioned Atalia.

'Yes, he does,' replied Alina. 'He's very excited about the whole project. He thinks people will come from all over Italy to see them.'

They turned another few corners and suddenly walked into a cave-like chamber with a deep passage running along the opposite side. To the left was a heavy wooden table and chairs that looked as if they should have been in a throne room of some sort. The ceiling was white and complete dome-like.

'What is this place?' asked Atalia.

'This is where it gets exciting,' replied Alina. 'This deep passage over here used to be a water passage. In the olden days, the people would use these water passages to do trade. People would bring boats along here and deliver goods and all sorts in these caverns. The local residents would meet here and receive the goods. They would then take them through the tunnels, like the ones we've just walked along, to their own businesses and homes.'

'Does that mean the hotel wasn't always a hotel?' asked Atalia.

'No, it wasn't,' replied Alina. 'Our hotel has been all sorts of businesses in the past. The history records we have show all this, but there is not so much information about the underground passages. In fact, I think I have pretty much told you everything I know.'

'What about the table and chairs?' asked Atalia, curious as to why these items would be there.

'Oh those,' laughed Alina. 'They've come down from the old banqueting room in the hotel. You didn't honestly think they were already here, did you, Atalia?'

Atalia felt embarrassed at her foolish question. 'No, of course not,' she said. 'But why are they here?'

'Oh, that's easy,' said Alina. 'Father sits down here and works. He often has meetings with others about the health and safety issues and how to ensure that people will be safe when they visit these caves. For example, a fence is going to be placed in front of the water passage so that no-one falls in there. He's very safety conscientious, you know.'

Atalia walked over to the table where Mr. Tonella had clearly left some of his folders and looked at the information. Inside the folder was a diagram mapping out the chambers and tunnels so far. Then there were the designs for ensuring the health and safety of the visitors, just as Alina had said.

'So what help do you want from me?' asked Atalia.

'There's some inscriptions on the walls,' replied Alina. 'We want to know what they say, and we thought that you might have the knowledge to understand the language'.

Atalia stared at the inscriptions. They initially looked as if they had been written in a language like Latin, but the more she looked at them, the more she realised that these words were not language as such, just mere annotations and markings that people had clearly made when these tunnels were bustling with activity.

'They are not really a language,' replied Atalia. 'They're more markings which people made at the time when these chambers and tunnels were in proper use. I will need to spend more time researching these marks to know more.'

'Oh,' said Alina, a little disappointed. 'I had been hoping that it was a secret code or something.'

'Afraid not,' replied Atalia. 'There's just this one word here that I need to check up on.' She continued to look around the chamber. Down the far end of the chamber was a metal gate that was padlocked with a number combination. Behind it was a tunnel of pure darkness.

'What's this gate about?' asked Atalia.

'Aah, that is the next part of the underground tunnels that Father is yet to explore. He put the gate in so that no-one would wander in there and get lost because there's no lights fitted in there yet. I think he knows that I would probably go wandering down there myself if I had a chance, so he's looking after me.'

Hmm... thought Atalia, *that tells me quite a lot about the sort of tenacious character that Alina has got.*

She took one more look around the cave before telling Alina that the time was getting late and that she ought to get home. It wasn't that she was scared. It was more the fact that she had seen what she came to see and could see no point in staying any longer.

*

'How did you get on with the secret caves?' asked Greta at breakfast the next morning.

'Yes, they were quite interesting. I have seen others like them in other parts of Tuscany.'

'Have you?' said Greta, quite surprised for she herself had never taken Atalia to see any caves.

'Yes,' replied Atalia. 'There are many of them in Tuscany and you can visit quite a lot of them in different places. The ones under the Tonellas' hotel are very similar.'

'So, you didn't see any cavemen?' said Jaq, jokingly.

'No,' chuckled Atalia. 'I did see one interesting word though.'

'What was that? Exit?' continued Jaq, trying to put together some cheap humour fairly quickly.

'No,' said Atalia. 'Jaq, it was more serious than that.'

Jaq's face immediately stopped being cheeky and took on a more serious countenance. 'Why, Atalia? What was it?'

Atalia took a piece of paper out of her pocket and handed it to Jaq.

'I wrote it down,' she said. 'I thought you would want to see it.'

Jaq opened the piece of paper and his eyes grew wide in astonishment. 'Does Alina know anything about this?' he asked.

'No, I didn't tell her. She wouldn't know anything about it anyway.'

Jaq looked at the piece of paper again, trying to now put everything he knew into context with the word that was now in front of him. It read 'Ardinghelli'.

Chapter 14

'Ardinghelli'... the word kept bouncing round and round Jaq's mind. *As he understood it, in Italian history, there had been two households in San Gimignano, much like the Capulets and Montagues in Shakespeare's 'Romeo and Juliet'. Like them, the two households had been in opposition to each other. On one hand you had the Ardinghellis and on the other hand you had the Salvuccis. These two families,* Jaq continued mulling, *both want to show their prominent power and wealth within the settlement of San Gimignano. To achieve this, both families went about building towers in the city with the intention that the highest tower showed the greatest family. But how did this fit with the secret tunnels under the Tonellas' hotel?*

'There's got to be a connection,' said Jaq, looking at Atalia frustratingly.

'My thought was that maybe the two families didn't just want prominence above the ground, but maybe under the ground as well,' suggested Atalia.

'Atalia, you could be right,' exclaimed Jaq. 'What if the power struggle was greater than that? They knew that if they controlled the tunnels then they held the control of San Gimignano. What do you think?'

'Maybe,' said Atalia. 'But where are you going to find the Salvucci name written up in the tunnels? Have you considered that maybe the name 'Ardinghelli' was there simply because that one particular family dealt with the water canal business?'

'Well, did they?' asked Jaq. 'Did the Ardinghellis deal with the water canals?'

'Well, Alina said they did,' replied Atalia.

'I see… and what about the Salvuccis?' Jaq was beginning to feel much more like an investigating detective who was running his ideas past his associate, a little like Sherlock Holmes and Watson.

'We don't know so much about the Salvuccis,' answered Atalia despondently. 'That's where Dino comes in. You need to find out more from him, Jaq.'

*

Jaq was immediately onto the case. He thought however that it might be better for Marco to ask Dino so it looked a little less obvious.

'But I can't do that,' said Marco. 'You know I am not good at conversations with teachers.'

'You can do it, Marco – I believe in you!'

'Why can't you do it, Jaq? You're the one whose interested in these Salvuccis. Besides which, I probably won't understand what Dino is telling me.'

'Just smile, nod your head, frown occasionally and give comments like…Hmm, that is interesting…and, How fascinating!'

'Hmm, that is interesting. How fascinating!' mimicked Marco with a silly expression on his face. 'It's not going to work, Jaq!'

'Yes, it is!' exclaimed Jaq. 'Look, Marco, I really need your help with this one. I wouldn't ask you if it wasn't really important. Now please help. I'll give you five euros for doing it.'

'Hmm, that is interesting…' said Marco again, much to Jaq's annoyance and entertainment. 'Okay, okay, I'll give it a go.'

'Thanks, Marco, you're a star! By the way, we'll hide a dictaphone in your pocket. That way you won't have to remember anything. I can just listen to it later.'

*

It took a few days before Marco had the opportunity to have a chat with Dino, which they did over lunch. Much to Jaq's irritation, there was a lot of the sound of munching and crunching of things like crisps in the recording and the occasional slurp of a drink. This meant that the conversation was a little broken, but Marco had done a good job in making himself sound convincing with his 'Hmm… that's interesting' (fifteen times) and 'How fascinating' (eighteen times). More importantly, Dino hadn't suspected anything.

*

'Jaq, can you stay behind after class please?' said Dino with quite an insistent tone of voice.

'Yes, Dino, sir…' replied Jaq quite puzzled.

'It's okay, Marco, you can go,' said Dino, pointing at the classroom door.

'What's the matter, sir?'

'It's about Marco,' replied Dino. 'He seems to be asking a lot of questions about the Salvuccis. Does he know anything about my connection to them?'

'I don't think so,' replied Jaq, trying to look all innocent. 'He never talks about it to me.'

'Oh,' replied Dino, looking quite surprised.

'I think it's probably that Marco is quite into his history topic at the moment, sir,' Jaq continued, attempting his biggest bluff to date. 'He's doing a project about historical modes of transport during the days of the Salvuccis and wondering whether they had any connections to the local water canals.'

'The Salvuccis…and the water canals?…' Dino looked puzzled. 'What a strange topic to be studying. No, the Salvuccis never had any involvement with the water canals at all. They were architects, not landscapers.'

'Oh…how fascinating,' said Jaq. 'I'll let Marco know so that he doesn't waste too much time trying to find incorrect information for his history topic. Can I go now, sir?'

'Yes…by all means,' replied Dino, escorting Jaq to the door and showing him out. 'Thank you'.

'No. Thank you, Dino,' replied Jaq with a grin across his face.

*

Jaq paid Marco his five euros and both boys laughed about the bluff of the history topic.

It was now time to tell Atalia the news. She wasn't surprised. She said that she also had found out that the Salvuccis weren't involved with the water canals and so that was the end of that mystery. Clearly the Ardinghellis had just put their name on the tunnels because they were involved in the trade that took place there. Nothing exciting after all.

'I do understand why Dino and Mr. Tonella ended up fighting that night at the tower though,' said Atalia. 'It's obvious. Mr. Tonella is clearly connected to the Ardinghellis and Dino is likewise connected to the Salvuccis. That night, they must have known that they both belonged to two different historical families and that's what caused the fight.'

'I agree,' said Jaq. 'But there must have been something more than that. Two grown men don't just start fighting because their relatives from centuries ago happened to be enemies.'

'No, that's true,' agreed Atalia. 'Still, tomorrow, we will know more.'

Jaq looked at Atalia with a confused look. 'Will we?' he enquired.

Atalia smiled and walked out of the living room.

*

It was Greta who was in for the greatest surprise the next morning, however. As usual, she had got up early ready to make the bread for that day. Being February, it could still be a little cold and dark when she got up, so she crept down the stairs with a shawl wrapped around her for additional warmth. After putting the dough into the oven, she sat down to make herself some breakfast. It was at this point that there was a knock on the front door. *How strange*, Greta thought, *no-one comes to the door this early – they know that the bread won't be ready yet.* She went to open the door.

Outside the door was a courier. He held in his hands a parcel wrapped in brown paper. It had an extravagant red bow on the top and a label hanging off the side, shaped in the style of a loaf of bread.

'Delivery for a 'Greta'' said the courier.

Greta frowned. She didn't know whether she approved of receiving an unexpected parcel or not. She closed the door and sat down on a chair at the kitchen table just staring at the parcel.

She couldn't actually remember having ever received a parcel before. *There certainly hadn't been any since her husband died and that was quite a while ago. Even Atalia had been living with them for… she wasn't sure. How long had Atalia been living with them? On one hand it felt like forever; but on the other hand, Atalia hadn't grown any taller, got any older or needed any new clothes because she had grown out of the last ones – so it couldn't have been that long, could it?*

When Jaq's footsteps could be heard coming down to breakfast, Greta hid the parcel in the cupboard under the sink. She didn't know why. She took it back out again when he had gone to school.

Greta was still staring at it when Atalia came downstairs. The stare was vacant, distant and emotionless.

'What is it?' asked Atalia inquisitively.

'I don't know,' replied Greta, coming around to reality. 'I haven't opened it yet.'

'Don't you think you ought to?' Atalia beckoned. 'Look, even the label is shaped like a loaf of bread. I expect it's a thank you from somebody. Does it say anything?'

Greta looked at the label. 'Nothing,' she replied.

'But look, someone's drawn a heart on the loaf of bread,' said Atalia, staring intently.

'Hmph,' replied Greta, walking away from the table and starting to wash the breakfast dishes in the sink. 'You open it, Atalia.'

Atalia took a deep breath and then carefully started undoing the Sellotape on the brown paper. She had never been the sort of person who simply ripped and tore at wrapping paper, which, in her opinion, was wasteful. By unwrapping the paper neatly, it could be used again.

Inside the parcel was a number of items. Atalia took them out one by one. First, there was a bag of bread flour – supposedly by the finest flour mill in the whole of Italy. Next, there was some yeast. This was followed by some salt, some sugar, (both wrapped in beautiful little cellophane wrappers) and some margarine (which had been placed in some kind of cooling container to prevent it from melting).

'Looks like someone has brought you some ingredients for making more bread,' said Atalia, pulling the last item out of the parcel which happened to be a jar of green olives.

Greta snorted. *Was this parcel a compliment or an insult? She tended to think it was the second. Clearly the person who had sent it thought that her bread was not good enough and therefore had sent through the ingredients for her to try and improve it with.*

'We shall throw it all away,' said Greta. 'I would not even give my friends these things. The insult of it.'

'Wait,' said Atalia. 'There's a piece of paper at the bottom with some writing on it.'

'Probably the recipe,' grumbled Greta. 'Get rid of it, Atalia.'

Atalia opened the piece of paper. This time it was her turn to look surprised. 'Umm, Greta, I think you ought to read it,' she said.

Greta snatched the piece of paper out of Atalia's hand furiously and started to read. As she did so though, her whole mood and countenance started to change. She stopped pacing around and sat herself down and re-read the letter to herself again. The expression on her face had gone from sheer indignation to surprise and then to a happy sort of embarrassment.

'Well I never,' said Greta. 'Atalia, we shall keep the ingredients and use them straightaway. Never before have I received such a wonderful compliment about my bread. This letter is medicine to the soul, Atalia.'

Her mood changed. 'The only thing I am puzzled about is who it's from. There's no name.'

'I think that's the idea,' smiled Atalia.

'What do you mean?'

'La Festa Degli Innamorati?' suggested Atalia.

Greta looked embarrassed. 'Valentine's Day?!'

Atalia nodded and pointed to the sign that hung over the oven in Greta's kitchen. It was written in Italian and read 'The way to a man's heart is through his stomach.'

Chapter 15

Jaq lay on his bed, wondering how it was that Atalia was so confident that they would know more the next day. He began recalling all the quirky details about this girl he had come to know as his sister. He couldn't quite remember how long she had been living with them, but it certainly been a while. *Clearly, Atalia was smart, witty, very knowledgeable – way beyond her years – and an extremely excellent help around the home. Indeed, she had made his mother very happy with no detriment to himself. Likewise, she had also helped <u>him</u> out on many occasions with assignments, research and homework.*

He remembered the time when he was the only one who knew who Franco Du Lupe was. He remembered the time when Greta had fallen off the balcony. He remembered the time he had been hiding in the garden and then found himself stuck outside. He also remembered about how Atalia had, in many respects, been strategic in bringing him and Alina together. But the more he thought about it, the more he realised that his sister (technically 'step-sister') was not your average person. *For a start she didn't ever seem to grow older or taller. Likewise, her clothes, whilst they did regularly get washed and dried, never seemed to get worn out. Her dress, for certain, looked as new as the day she had first worn it.*

A lightning bolt of a thought suddenly struck him. *Perhaps Atalia would never grow older. She would be like Peter Pan or something. He, Greta, Alina, Dino, Mr. and Mrs. Tonella, everyone in San Gimignano would get old, bent and grey, but Atalia wouldn't? The thought didn't see possible. He could imagine himself as an old man with his childish sister looking after him, talking of the times when he had been young too.*

'No, no, no…' Jaq exclaimed. 'I can't think like this…'

Yet his mind went back to a Neverland mentality where he could see Atalia being something like a sister or cousin to Peter Pan. *Perhaps she was like Mary Poppins and came to help people like him have a bit more happiness in life. Perhaps she was…*

'No, no, stop it!' Jaq told himself. The realms of his imagination were going too far. He took a deep breath before lecturing himself about how Atalia was only a girl who had been brought to his family with a request to be looked after. They had kindly taken her in, and she had become part of the family. There was nothing more to it. The fact that she was an intelligent girl was insignificant.

But then, what about the database that couldn't find her on the system?... No, it could be as simple an explanation as the fact that the hospital records of Atalia's birth had somehow got caught up in a computer blip or error.

The question was: should he continue to accept Atalia for who she was, or should he try and find out more about his mysterious sister? He didn't know. *On one hand, it wouldn't make much difference anyway – life would continue. On the other hand, it would be quite intriguing.*

*

When the next day did come, a letter arrived in the post. Greta rushed to the door. Jaq noted how unusual it was for his mother to rush. It was almost as if she was expecting something to arrive. When Greta looked at the envelopes, she gave out a smile before quickly disappearing into the living room with the letter and an envelope opener.

'What was all that about?' Jaq asked Atalia.

'A personal letter I guess...' she replied.

'I've never seen my mum rush to open a letter before,' said Jaq.

'I think I've got a good idea who it may be from although I don't know who.'

'That makes absolutely no sense at all, Atalia,' exclaimed Jaq.

'I mean, I think I know the sort of person it is from, but I don't know their name,' replied Atalia.

'Go on then,' said Jaq impatiently. 'Who is it from?'

'The person who sent the parcel?' suggested Atalia.

Jaq thought for a moment. 'Oh, I see…' His eyes now realising what Atalia meant. 'You think it's a secret admirer.'

'Well, I don't think it's a bread order,' she replied sarcastically.

Greta's face reappeared at the door. 'Atalia,' she said, 'I have something to show you.'

'Told you!' Atalia smirked at Jaq. 'Coming…' she replied to Greta.

With that, Atalia left the kitchen and went into the living room, closing the door behind her. Jaq went and put his ear to the door and could hear nothing, but whispered voices and they weren't loud enough for him to make out the words.

*

Alina was waiting for Jaq outside the school hall when lunch was commencing.

'Jaq, could I talk to you?' she said.

Jaq's face looked worried. 'Is there something the matter?' he asked.

'No…' Alina replied. 'I just want to have a chat with you…alone!'

Jaq nodded his head contemplatively and together they walked towards the back of the baseball court where they found a small bush to sit beside and have their lunch.

Jaq thought he knew what was coming next. He feared the worst but braced himself to take the news that would break his heart.

'I wanted to talk to you about Dino,' Alina began.

'What?!' exclaimed Jaq. 'Why do you want to talk about him?'

'Because he clearly likes archaeology and he might know some information that would be helpful,' said Alina innocently.

'Oh…' said Jaq, his mind both relieved that the news hadn't been what he had anticipated, but also puzzled over Alina's sudden interest in archaeology. 'Why don't you talk to him yourself?'

'Aah, that's tricky,' said Alina. 'I'm not in one of his classes and it might seem a little strange for me to be asking him about a subject I don't study.'

'Why do you want to know about archaeology anyway?' asked Jaq.

'Well, I found some strange writing on the tunnels underneath the hotel and I wondered if he might know more about the language,' Alina continued. 'I did ask Atalia, but she didn't seem to know anything.'

Alina put her arm in Jaq's. 'Please help me, Jaq.' Jaq had the feeling that not everything was quite adding up, but there seemed no reason why he couldn't at least ask Dino for some information.

'Okay,' he replied. 'What do I say to Dino?'

Alina pulled out a photo and handed it to him. 'Just ask him if he knows anything about this.'

Jaq looked at the photo. There was nothing exciting about it – just some old stone walls and an underground water canal. 'Seems simple enough,' he said.

'There's just one more thing…' started Alina. 'Please don't let Dino know I asked. Make him believe that it was you asking. Please, Jaq, please!'

Her puppy-dog eyes pleading with his heart prevented him from resisting her request. 'Okay, I'll do it,' Jaq replied. 'Only it won't be today. I don't see Dino until tomorrow.'

'That's fine,' replied Alina. 'I can wait until then.' She gave Jaq a kiss on the cheek before getting up and walking back over to the school building, waving to some friends on the way.

Jaq sat there. For a moment he wasn't sure what had happened. He thought about it. *He had just agreed to ask Dino for information about a photo, hadn't he? There was no problem in that, was there?... No, of course not.* Yet something in Jaq's heart felt that there was more to this request – he just couldn't put his finger on it.

'Why are girls so complicated?' he asked Marco later that day.

'Don't ask me,' said Marco. 'You're the one who got yourself caught up with Alina.'

'Hmph,' replied Jaq.

*

When the evening came, Jaq found Atalia sat on the sofa reading a book.

'Well, we didn't find out any more like you said we would,' hinted Jaq.

'Yes, we did,' replied Atalia, her eyes still on the words of her book.

'What?!' demanded Jaq. 'What did we find out?'

'We found out that neither the Salvuccis nor the Ardinghellis built the Devil's Tower in the town.'

'How did we find that out?' asked Jaq, wondering why he was still using the word 'we' in the sentence.

'Because it says so in this book,' replied Atalia. 'The builders of the Devil's Tower are unknown. I've been doing my research.'

'So where does that put things?' enquired Jaq.

'That means,' Atalia continued, 'we have two men both interested in a tower that neither of their ancestors built.'

Jaq pondered the thought for a moment. 'So there has got to be some reason why they are both so interested in the tower?'

Atalia nodded. 'Come on, Jaq…think about it…why would two men whose ancestors built some of the largest towers in the town both be interested in the largest tower of all?'

'They want to know who built the tallest one?' Jaq suggested.

Atalia shook her head. 'No, it has to be more than that.'

Jaq pulled Alina's photo out of his trouser pocket where it had been for the majority of the day. 'Does this help?' he asked.

'Where did this come from?' Atalia enquired.

'Alina gave it to me today. She wants me to ask Dino what he knows about the archaeology from this photo.'

'Does she?' asked Atalia with a smirk. 'Well, let's see what he says, shall we?'

Jaq looked at Atalia. She had that look on her face that suggested that she knew something he didn't. He was going to ask her but decided not to. He felt quite tired, so he took himself upstairs to get changed into his pyjamas.

Atalia closed her book and stared at the dancing flames of the fire. The embers sparked and the wood cracked. Reds, yellow and oranges spat into the air. It was if the flames were doing a dangerous dance of passion and violence. Something that perhaps described the Salvuccis and the Ardinghellis.

*

The next morning another letter arrived for Greta. It was in the same handwriting as the one the day before. Once again, Greta snatched at it and took it off into the living room to read it. Once again, Atalia was summoned in to see it too. Jaq stood outside the door perplexed and yet bemused.

'What does that letter say?' he asked Atalia. 'You know, the one that arrives in the morning.'

'It's a letter complimenting your mum on how brilliant a baker she is,' replied Atalia.

'But that's not all, is it?' suggested Jaq.

'No… she's got a secret admirer. He says that he cannot wait to see her again and that it will be sometime soon. It's made Greta very excited. I just hope she's not too disappointed when he comes.'

'Why would she be disappointed?' Jaq asked.

'Because his Italian doesn't seem to be brilliant,' replied Atalia. 'That's why Greta calls me in – she needs me to work out and decipher what doesn't make sense.'

'But why is that a problem?' Jaq asked naively.

'Jaq…he's not a local person. Everyone who lives around here is Italian. They speak Italian. This man doesn't. That means he is a tourist!'

'So?…'

'Come on, Jaq. How would you feel if you had an admirer who cared for you, but comes from outside of your community?'

'Well, people of all different nationalities get together, don't they? We live in a multi-cultural world.'

'Yes, Jaq…but this is Italy. Not only that, but this is a small community in Italy. This is San Gimignano.'

Jaq nodded. He understood what Atalia was getting at. He wished her goodnight and wandered his way up the stairs to his bedroom, the end of his dressing gown belt trailing along the staircase behind him.

Don't worry Jaq, Atalia thought to herself, it won't be long now. Soon everything will make sense. I know it will.

With that, Atalia wished Greta goodnight, went upstairs, fetched her little bag with the two sticks and twelve stones inside, and went out into the back garden.

Chapter 16

It wasn't long before the whole town of San Gimignano knew about the mysterious letters that Greta was receiving as she had told all of her friends, relatives, neighbours and clients. In true Italian style, the news had then been passed from one to another and then another until there wasn't a resident of the town who didn't know. Every tourist buying Greta's bread, who wasn't from another part of Italy, became a suspect. The gossip around the town varied from the letters coming from a man who was fat, slim, tall, short, young old, athletic, lazy, good-looking, rather unattractive, intelligent, simplistic; and whose job was a doctor, a teacher, a carpenter, a stonemason, a shop assistant, a diplomat, an artist, a professional actor, an author, a baker, etc. to even some of the most extraordinary ideas of the person being a world famous athlete, the world's strongest man, a famous television celebrity and so it went on. Not only that, but the nationalities also changed: he was French, German, American, Australian, Hungarian, British, Spanish, Russian…virtually every country on the map had got a mention. The wildest rumour of all was that a piece of Greta's bread had been taken on a flight by Jonita, the local solicitor, to Argentina. He supposedly hadn't eaten it but offered it to a gentleman who was extremely hungry and needed it. The gentleman himself had been so impressed by the quality of the bread that he had insisted upon finding the woman who would become the love of his life. The rich relatives, seeing how poor he was, had paid for him to fly to San Gimignano to find the bread-maker who would change his life forever. Of course, Jonita denied the whole story – and everyone knew it to be completely farcical – but it still made for a good rumour.

Surprisingly, Greta found it all rather entertaining. It gave her lots of opportunities to chit-chat and her contacts list had grown considerably. Not only that, but her sales of bread had also gone up so quickly that Greta had advertised for another person to come and help her. She quickly interviewed Klaudina who had relocated to San Gimignano from Sardinia. She became quickly accepted into the community simply because she was working for Greta. If Greta had chosen Klaudina, then everything must be fine and therefore everyone liked and trusted her.

The letters continued to arrive nearly every day and Greta studied them carefully, always turning a pinky-red colour in her cheeks with an ever-increasing smile on her face.

'Don't you wish that you knew who they were from?' asked Jaq, slightly frustrated by the whole scenario.

'We shall know over time,' said Greta. 'You don't seriously think that this person is going to write to me forever without making himself known, do you Jaq?'

Jaq took the point. Yes, it did seem a little mad really, but he supposed that Greta was right – it was a matter of time before the mysterious admirer would make themselves known. It was good, however, to see his mother looking so happy. He just hoped she wouldn't be too disappointed when the actual writer did appear.

*

Life at school for Jaq had been quite pressurised. His final exams were coming up in the months ahead and he wanted to do well.

'Have you thought about what you're going to do after the exams?' Marco asked him.

'No…not really. I just want to do really well in my exams first,' replied Jaq.

'Well, I know what I want to do,' said Marco.

'Let me guess…um…basketball?' said Jaq with that all-knowing look on his face.

'How did you know?' replied Marco, looking quite surprised.

'Just a hunch.'

'Apparently my family have said that I will need to go to a sporting college in Turin. They say we might have to relocate.'

'I would miss you, Marco,' began Jaq 'But…'

'It's fine though,' continued Marco, totally oblivious to Jaq's reply. 'My father is looking for a new house already. It takes about six months to move you know, so if we are going to get there in time for college to start then we've got to get a move on.'

'Have you been given a place at the college then?'

'No! Not yet,' answered Marco, 'but they will take me with no problems at all.' He tossed his basketball into the air and it landed straight into the basket. 'See? Easy!'

Jaq told Marco that he wished him the best of luck and started wandering off home. He hadn't really thought about his future before. *Normally you would either go off to study or you would take on the family business from your father.* In Jaq's case neither were really a possibility – *he certainly didn't want to carry on studying, and he didn't have a father to take a business on from. As for baking bread like his mother, this was not a future he could bear to imagine. Besides which, Greta now had Klaudina to take over the business one day. If not, Atalia could take it on,* he thought. He couldn't realistically however imagine Atalia being able to what with staying so young and having greater intelligence than just baking bread.

'What do you think I should do?' he asked Alina.

'Marry me,' she replied.

'I meant, what future work should I try and do?' he said, smiling at her light-hearted comment.

'I don't know, Jaq – but whatever you decide to do, I still think you should marry me when we are old enough.' She made a cute face at him and Jaq smiled and hugged her back. 'Okay…'

This conversation however hadn't helped Jaq get any further inspiration for his future. *Should he become a philosopher like Franco Du Lupe? Or a teacher like Dino? A solicitor like Jonita? Or a businessman like Mr. Tonella?* He didn't know. He would need time to think and ponder on it.

*

Alina, however, had likewise been putting some careful thought to Jaq's dilemma too. She was determined that whatever Jaq's future was going to be, she was going to be the wonderful wife next to him. Therefore, she decided that it was only right that she should try and ensure that Jaq had a good future ahead of him. *After all, the daughter of a successful business man and hotelier couldn't expect to be married to someone who didn't hold some position or respect within the town. No, she would think of something and ensure that Jaq was more than suitable and prepared for being successful and a good husband.*

Alina spoke to her father. 'Father, what do you think of Jaq, Greta's son?' she blurted out over the dinner table one evening.

'Well, if he's anything like Greta, then he's a fine young man. I know that you like him, Alina,' Mr. Tonella replied.

'I was wondering if he could come and work for us,' suggested Alina with a bit of a pleading tone in her voice. 'When he's finished school, I mean. I could teach him everything he needs to know, and I am sure that he would make an excellent worker. He's very kind and patient, good with people...' She felt herself beginning to ramble and her face blush.

Mr. Tonella looked at his daughter. *Clearly, Jaq meant a lot to her and he would never want to do anything that wouldn't make her happy.*

'He can come and work for us if he wants to,' said Mr. Tonella. 'I am not quite sure what position we will give him yet, but if he's as marvellous as you say he is, I am sure that we can find him something. Perhaps he could answer the phone on reception.'

'Great,' replied Alina. 'I shall let him know right away. I think that he ought to come and have a good tour of the hotel as well so that he gets to know everything about it.'

'Don't get too carried away with the idea,' said Mrs. Tonella. 'Let's see what Jaq feels about the whole concept first, shall we?'

Alina looked at her mother's stare, realised that she was right, but decided to dismiss it. There was no reason in Alina's mind why Jaq wouldn't instantly want to accept the job and start the day after school finished. *After all, he would be with her all day. Perhaps one day, he would even take over the hotel from her father and it would become the 'Tonella and Alfonsi Hotel'.*

*

Jaq was not immediately struck with the idea of working at the hotel. He was a little nervous of Mr. Tonella who seemed to do everything with a high level of efficiency, accuracy and meticulously. This wasn't Jaq's normal style. He preferred something steady, easy-going and comparatively relaxing. The hotel industry didn't seem quite the idea.

Alina however continued to chatter on and on about how great it would be and what a success they could make of the whole hotel. Perhaps they could introduce great concert evenings or national events to the hotel.

Jaq was convinced that Alina was letting her imagination run away with her.

'Do come over to the hotel and have a look around,' said Alina. 'Then you can see what you think and tell my father what position you think you would like. Perhaps you could be the porter. We haven't got a porter at the moment.'

'If you think I am going to stand outside all day, wearing a silly outfit, and waiting for someone to arrive with loads of luggage, then you've got another thing coming,' said Jaq. 'This is San Gimignano, Alina, not Rome.'

'I know that,' retorted Alina, 'but we do get a lot of summer business with all the tourists and they've always got lots of luggage. But if you don't fancy that, what about working in the bar?'

The thought of working in the hotel bar suddenly captured Jaq's imagination. *That would be alright – wait until someone comes and asks for a drink, pour it out for them, take the money, give the change…easy. Now that didn't sound like hard work at all.*

'Alright, I will come and have a look around,' said Jaq.

'Great!' exclaimed Alina. 'I shall tell my father straight away. See you at seven.' With that she ran off, leaving Jaq alone on the doorstep of his house.

*

'Mum,' shouted Jaq as he came in the door. 'I'm going to the Tonella's hotel this evening to have a look around. What should I wear?'

'Something smart, son,' replied Greta, wondering why Jaq was going to the Tonella's.

'Alina thinks that Mr. Tonella is going to give me a job when I finish school,' said Jaq. 'It sounds alright to me.'

'I'm glad you think so,' said Greta. 'At least you will be working, Jaq. I was rather worried that you would be at home under my feet all day.'

Jaq laughed but inwardly knew that Greta's statement would have been true had Alina not said anything to Mr. Tonella. He went upstairs, emptied his entire wardrobe all over the floor, before selecting what he thought would be suitable. After taking a shower, he put on a pair of white trousers, a blue open-necked shirt and a beige jacket. Next, he combed his hair very carefully, cleaned his shoes and went downstairs.

'You're looking very smart,' said Atalia. 'Where are you going?'

'To the Tonella's,' replied Jaq with a grin on his face. 'I am going for a tour of the hotel.'

'With Alina I guess,' said Atalia.

'Of course,' smiled Jaq, 'but then Mr. Tonella is hopefully going to give me a job for when I finish school.'

'Well, let's hope he doesn't get you washing up the dirty plates in the kitchen,' retorted Atalia. 'Not to say that the extra practice would help,' she joked.

Jaq's face looked horrified for a moment. *Working in the kitchens?* His mind hadn't even imagined that the kitchens were a possibility. He could see himself slaving over a sink of pots and pans that were all sticky, mucky and burnt.

No, he thought to himself, *if Mr. Tonella says about the kitchen work, I shall have to tell him that I am not interested in the job.*

Greta and Atalia watched Jaq from the window as he walked off down the street to the Tonella's hotel with his head held high and his steps being placed quite firmly and deliberately.

'I never imagined I would see the day when Jaq took life so seriously,' said Greta.

'It's only because of Alina,' replied Atalia.

'Yes… I know that, Atalia. It's just that all of a sudden Jaq seems to be growing up.'

*

The only thing that Jaq could seem to talk about from his evening at the hotel was the bar. Mr. Tonella had given him the opportunity to try serving the customers and pouring the drinks. Jaq had flourished in the role and Mr. Tonella had most definitely offered Jaq a job as a barman once he had finished school. He would work from four o clock in the afternoon until midnight. *This,* Jaq thought, *was ideal as it meant that he didn't have to get up early in the morning.* Alina, likewise, was delighted. Jaq would now be around the hotel every day.

'What did you think of the tunnels, Jaq?' Atalia asked him later when Greta wasn't around.

'I thought they were alright, but I wouldn't want to spend too much time down there. Mr. Tonella certainly seems to have some sort of plans for them. Maybe he wants to create a whole set of businesses down there or something?'

That was a thought that hadn't crossed Atalia's mind before. Surely not though.

'Did you show Dino the photo that Alina gave you?'

'Yes,' replied Jaq. 'He said that it looked quite interesting and he took a photocopy of it. He hasn't said anything else since. But Alina certainly wasn't happy when I told her.'

'Did she say why?' enquired Atalia.

'No, only the fact that she hoped he didn't know where it came from,' Jaq replied. He sat down on the sofa in the living room and turned the television on. 'I used to think that there was something mysterious about Dino and Mr. Tonella,' he continued, 'but now I have been at the hotel, I think that Mr. Tonella's just trying to do something with the tunnels he has found under his hotel. Dino, on the other hand, is just obsessed with the Devil's Tower. Two men with two different interests…nothing to worry about.'

Atalia stood staring at Jaq for a minute or two. She realised that within one day, Jaq's priorities had taken a sudden change. No longer was he interested in the mysteries of life. Now he was going to be a bar attender and eventually a husband to Alina. Still, never mind, Atalia thought to herself, I came to San Gimignano to solve a problem and solve it, I will.

Chapter 17

Jaq's approach to school work took a sudden change. The offer from Mr. Tonella to work as a bar attender had made Jaq realise that he needed to work hard and achieve some great results. Mr. Tonella had, in Jaq's mind, become an icon – *someone to look up to, someone to aspire to become, someone who seemingly had it all – wealth, health, family, business...* as far as Jaq was concerned, that was all that mattered.

'Haven't you ever dreamt of become successful, Atalia?' he said one morning at breakfast.

'Atalia is successful,' grunted back Greta, who was busy washing dishes, and determined to reply before Atalia spoke. 'Look at how intelligent she is – that makes her successful.'

'Success isn't about intelligence, mum,' exclaimed Jaq. 'Success is about being rich, having position and having your own business, and that kind of thing. I was merely asking Atalia if she wanted to be successful.'

'If the definition of success is your definition, Jaq, then it doesn't interest me.'

'What?!' cried Jaq. 'You can't be serious, Atalia!'

'My definition of success is different,' Atalia replied calmly.

'Well, go on then,' said Jaq tauntingly, 'what's your definition of success?'

Atalia thought for a moment. 'Success,' she started, 'is making a monumental difference to the world in the interest of improving other peoples' daily life experiences.' She paused. 'Isn't that what you want, Jaq?'

Jaq nodded his head bluffingly. In truth, he had no idea what Atalia's answer meant, but he didn't want to make himself look ignorant. Greta however could read him like a book.

'Put it simply for Jaq, Atalia – he doesn't get it,' she said.

Atalia thought again. 'It means that success is about making the world a better place by helping people to develop and enjoy their everyday lives.'

'See, I was right,' blurted out Jaq. 'You need to have money to do that – therefore you have to be successful by my definition.'

'Not quite,' replied Atalia. 'My definition of success can be achieved without money, without business and without position. My definition can be achieved by anyone. Even a very young child can be very successful as can a very old person too.'

'Hmm…I don't get you, Atalia – some of your ideas are weird.'

The conversation stopped abruptly. Greta simply carried on washing up. Atalia continued eating her breakfast whilst Jaq sat at the table playing with the spoon, avoiding eye contact with Atalia. He knew that she was probably right about success, but certainly didn't want to admit it.

Greta interrupted the silence after a short while.

'Jaq, what are you doing about the after-school revision classes?'

'I'm not going to do them,' replied Jaq casually.

'I thought you wanted to do well in your exams,' said Greta.

'I do,' said Jaq, 'but I figure that rather than attending different revision classes every night for different subjects, it would be easier to do it at home.'

Greta and Atalia stared at him. The whole concept of Jaq sat at home with piles of books around him studying was almost inconceivable.

'Yes...I thought that maybe Atalia could help me just revise the parts I don't know. After all, I hate to admit it, but she does know everything.'

*

Atalia had been very flattered by Jaq's compliment. She was more than happy to help him, of course. The sessions started almost immediately, and Greta was delighted to see both of them sat together, talking through various subjects from History to Geography to Maths to Science to Philosophy to Religious Studies. Jaq was surprisingly very grateful and soon adjusted to Atalia being his home tutor. The fact that she was still younger than him didn't really cross his mind.

When the final revision examinations took place, Jaq's teachers were amazed by his predicted results, particularly as all of them had noted that Jaq hadn't attended any of the revision classes. Dino was the most surprised. Jaq's understanding of Philosophy seemed to have just come on remarkably. He noted that Jaq was now very confident to talk about some of the more difficult subjects, such as the dying speech of Socrates, and the Cosmological Argument for the existence of God. He wondered whether Jaq had somehow been cheating.

'How is it that you are doing so well?' he asked Jaq.

'Because I have studied hard,' replied Jaq. 'Mr. Tonella has offered me a job so I want to do well so that I can be successful.'

Dino looked at him suspiciously. 'You know I don't like Mr. Tonella,' he commented, 'but that's not the point. Somehow you are doing well without the revision classes. How are you doing it?'

'I study at home for a couple of hours each night,' said Jaq. 'If you don't believe me, ask Alina. She will tell you that I only see her at the weekends because I am studying every evening.'

Dino raised his eyebrows, wiped his brow and admitted defeat. He didn't believe Jaq, but he also couldn't deny the results that Jaq was achieving.

'Well, let's see what happens in the actual exams, shall we?' said Dino.

'Yes, Dino. By the way, did you have any more thoughts about that photo I showed you?'

'Yes…' replied Dino, his face lighting up. 'I wondered if you knew where the photo was taken.'

'Underneath the Tonella's hotel,' replied Jaq before suddenly realising that Alina had told him not to say anything. 'Err… I mean I think that there may be tunnels running under the bottom end of San Gimignano.'

Dino looked both interested and disappointed.

'Okay, Jaq…keep up the good work…' said Dino. 'I have more exam papers to mark.' He picked up his bag and walked out of the room.

*

Three days later, Jaq was sat in the living room with Atalia revising more philosophy. Greta was sat in the kitchen reading a book about pizza making; and sipping a glass of red wine. There was a knock on the door. Greta put down her book and glass and went to answer it.

Outside the door stood Dino. 'Excuse me, Greta, but is Jaq at home?'

'Yes, he's studying in the living room,' replied Greta. 'Shall I get him for you?'

'No, no,..' replied Dino quietly. 'I wanted to pop in and talk to you about his results.'

'Well, I believed that he was doing well,' replied Greta quite indignantly.

'Well, he is,' replied Dino. 'That's what confuses me. That's why I popped around. Jaq told me that he was revising every evening.'

'Well, he has been studying,' replied Greta, becoming more indignant with Dino. 'Have you anything else you need to say?'

'Well, no…' replied Dino. 'I just don't know how he's doing it.'

At that very moment, Atalia walked into the kitchen. 'Oh sorry,' she replied. 'I was just coming to get something. I can come back later.'

'No, no, it's fine, Atalia,' said Greta. 'Dino's just going.'

Dino took a step back and watched as Atalia went to the kitchen drawer and took out a sieve and a wooden spoon.

'Listen, Jaq,' she said, 'Aristotle said…' Her words faded away as she closed the living room door.

Dino stood speechless.

'Are you going now, Dino?' said Greta, her hands on her hips. She felt that Dino had already prolonged his seemingly unnecessary stay and wanted to get him out of the house as quickly as possible.

'Did I just hear her talk about Aristotle?' asked Dino.

'I think that's what she said,' replied Greta. 'I wasn't listening.'

'But...but...she shouldn't know anything about Aristotle at her age,' said Dino, 'let alone explain something like him to Jaq.'

'Atalia knows more than you could imagine,' replied Greta. 'Now, with no offence, Dino, but could you kindly leave and let us get on in peace.'

'Yes...yes...of course...' said Dino, still bewildered by what he had witnessed. Was it possible that this young girl was teaching Jaq and that was how he was doing so well? It didn't seem possible.

*

Greta's secret admirer letters had continued to come daily. Each one promised her of a wonderful life that she could have if she continued to bake such wonderful bread. Greta began to wonder if this secret admirer was going to offer her a business proposition. But it wasn't long before she received a most intriguing letter.

The letter had arrived in the usual style of envelope. Greta opened it, but rather than there being a letter inside, there was an invitation. It read:

To the wonderful breadmaker of my life,

It is time that I saw you in person and to make my identity known. As you know I have admired your skill for a long time. Now I wish to admire the lady herself.

Would you please give me the honour of meeting me for dinner at Tonella's hotel this evening? I have booked a table for seven forty-five.

I look forward to seeing you.

Enzo.

'Enzo?' said Greta. 'What kind of a name is that? Enzo.'

Atalia agreed that the name certainly sounded unusual. Greta however spent the rest of the day in a kind of daydream. The name 'Enzo' would be uttered quietly from her lips. Atalia found observing Greta's reaction all very amusing.

'I will leave you to cook dinner for Jaq and yourself,' said Greta to Atalia. 'I know that you can cook well. If you want, you can make a Gorgonzola pasta – Jaq particularly likes that dinner. I must get ready to see Enzo.'

She danced around the kitchen, out the door, up the stairs and to her room. An hour later she reappeared wearing a long, royal blue dress, heeled shoes, a smart jacket, a neck-piece and some amazing jewellery.

'Wow,' said Atalia, most amazed at how beautiful Greta looked. 'You look amazing!'

'Thank you, Atalia. Dinner at the Tonellas is clearly a very special occasion so I want to look my best.'

She kissed both Jaq and Atalia on the cheeks and wished them both a good night. She didn't know what time she would be home…

*

'I am meeting someone,' said Greta when she arrived at the hotel.

Mr. Tonella appeared from another doorway. 'Ah, Greta – good to see you this evening. I believe you are having dinner with a Mr. Enzo. He's waiting for you on table 22.'

Greta followed Mr. Tonella to the dining room and gazed around, looking for a gentleman sat by himself. There were a few so she couldn't be certain which one Enzo would be. She desperately hoped that it wasn't the old man with the long white beard and the hideous number of wrinkles. A sigh of relief came as Mr. Tonella led her past the old man, who simply smiled and gave her a wink.

At table 22 sat an elegant gentleman wearing a smart navy-blue suit and a pale-yellow shirt and tie. He had a black beard and a curly moustache. His black curly hair was impeccably combed and sprayed, Greta noted. Her immediate thought was that he was extremely handsome and probably in his late 50's.

The man stood up and took Greta's hand. 'Good evening, most beautiful lady, my name is Enzo.'

Greta introduced herself and they both sat down for dinner. The rest of the evening went by in a flash as both of them enjoyed the meal, chatted continuously with many fits of laughter in between. Anyone being a fly on the wall would have thought that the two of them were old friends who had known each other for years.

*

'What happened?' asked Atalia the next morning.

'It was the best evening of my life,' replied Greta. 'Enzo is such a wonderful man. He's one of the leading bakers in the whole of France.'

Atalia paused and thought for a moment. 'Not the one who bought the bread when I was new here,' she said. 'Do you remember I told you about him? He had black curly hair and a black beard and moustache...'

'Yes...that's him,' replied Greta very excitedly.

'Well, what did he want? Is he offering you a job in France?'

'No,' said Greta. 'He's moving to San Gimignano. He's staying at the Tonellas Hotel until he buys a property.'

'Why is he coming to San Gimignano?' enquired Jaq quite suspiciously.

'Apparently he has a business associate here who he is hoping to work with very closely.'

'And do you know who that person is?' asked Jaq curiously.

'No…I didn't think to ask,' said Greta. 'It's none of my business after all.'

'Oh, that's where I think you are mistaken,' said Atalia with an all-knowing look in her face. 'What job does he do?'

'I told you, he's a baker,' said Greta, still not understanding where the conversation was going.

'And who is the best baker in San Gimignano?' asked Atalia, trying hard to lead Greta to the right conclusions.

'Um…you don't mean?' She looked at Atalia and Jaq's faces. 'You mean…? No, surely not. Work with me?!'

Atalia and Jaq nodded.

'You're the one he wanted to meet for dinner,' said Jaq.

'Yes…well…umm…' started Greta all in a fluster. 'Well I shall ask him next time I see him.'

'And when would that be?' enquired Atalia.

'Tonight,' said Greta abruptly. 'I shall ask him tonight!'

Chapter 18

Enzo stood outside the Tonella's hotel wearing his long tailored grey coat with six bronze buttons all glistening with the reflection of the street lamp. He rubbed his fingers together to keep them warm on what was a comparatively chilly evening due to the strong winds that had been blowing that day. His hair was neatly combed back and his moustache beautifully trimmed. His purple and blue neckerchief concealed the brand-new white shirt he had bought that day for the occasion of meeting with Greta Alfonsi for their second dinner date. He looked at his Rolex watch and saw that he was being impatient – there was still four more minutes to go before they were due to meet.

Greta was not one for being late. She had learnt that time was of the essence and that every moment should be taken advantage of, for each and every minute of her life would never come again. Seize the day, she told herself. Make every minute count.

She too had made herself look very presentable with some clothes that had been sat in her wardrobe, waiting for the right occasion. She put on a long grey dress, a pale rose-pink jacket, a grey scarf and her favourite Gucci perfume. Tonight was an important night. It was the night to find out whether Enzo had travelled all the way to San Gimignano just for her.

*

Dino sat and pondered in his chair for hours. His wife had tried cooking him his favourite meal of spaghetti bolognaise, but even this hadn't taken him out of his puzzled thoughts. He couldn't make it out – how was a young girl like Atalia teaching her older brother so well? Jaq's results had certainly improved, he couldn't deny it, but why did this girl have such a knowledge? It certainly had nothing to do with the school as she wasn't even a pupil there.

He manoeuvred the spaghetti around his plate.

'Aren't you going to eat that?' asked Mrs. Salvucci.

'Sorry…what?' replied Dino.

His wife muttered something in Italian and threw her apron down on the table and marched out of the room.

Dino knew that, somehow, he had to find out more about Atalia. Asking Jaq would be pointless and rather too obvious. No, he needed to find out for himself. Perhaps, he thought, he could offer her some tutoring and then ask some leading questions. No…stupid thought, he told himself, she seems to know everything anyway. Perhaps… the word got stuck on his lips, mainly because he didn't know how to finish the sentence. There had to be someway of finding out about Atalia's intelligence.

*

The brainwave hit Dino about 3am in the morning. *The tower. It was obvious. If Atalia was as clever as it seems that she was, she would know information about the Devil's Tower. By asking her for information about the tower, he would find out just how clever she was – not only that though, but he might just discover some answers that he had been searching for. If Atalia could answer those questions, then he would know the truth of the history of the Devil's Tower and hopefully be able to prove once and for all that the tower had indeed been built by the Salvucci family.*

His imagination went into overdrive. He imagined Atalia stood by the tower telling him that this tower had been build by his ancestors and that the tower would forever be owned by the future generations of Salvuccis. *Dino would then get recognition from across the town of being the legitimate and rightful owner of a tower whose ownership had been questioned for years. Atalia would prove it in front of the local and national authorities with her exceptional knowledge and various pieces of paper that proved it to be so. Admittedly he wouldn't know where these papers had come from, but that wouldn't matter. There would be a whole town celebration, and everyone would honour him. In fact, he would probably be made the next town mayor of San Gimignano – and his children would continue in his stead when he became too old to continue any more. His family would once again be forever engraved in the Italian history books.*

He paused, glad that he hadn't declared his thoughts out loud, for in doing so he would have told those hearing all that he had hoped for. Still, his secret wasn't out and no-one need know. He wouldn't even tell Atalia. All she needed to know was that he wanted to know more about the Devil's Tower from an archaeological background.

His mind flitted again. *What if Atalia didn't know as much as she appeared to know? What if it could never be proved that the tower had originally been built by the Salvucci family? Or worse still, what if the Ardinghelli family had built the tower? That would mean that if the Tonellas found out, they would lay claim to the tower and their names would forever be written in the history books.*

His imagination stirred again as he pictured Mr. Tonella taking all the glory that he should have. *He saw Mr. Tonella riding a white horse through the centre of San Gimignano with all the people heralding him as the new town mayor. He saw himself stood in the crowds as Mr. Tonella rode by. The horse stopped and Mr. Tonella turned and looked scornfully at Dino, laughing at his hopelessness. Alina Tonella would be walking alongside the horse and look at him with this look of 'you're just a teacher'. His own children stood at his side, looking up at him, their father, wondering why they weren't the ones who were dressed in fine clothes and having the wealth and admiration of the village.*

'NOOOOOOOOOO!' Dino cried out. His wife and children came rushing into the kitchen.

'What's the matter, dear?' asked Mrs. Salvucci.

'Oh,…oh….nothing…' said Dino, coming back to reality. 'I'm sorry…my mind was somewhere else.'

'Well I wish it would come back here,' replied Mrs. Salvucci. 'Now, come on, eat your dinner and take your mind off whatever it is you are worrying about.'

'Yes,' said Dino humbly. 'Yes, that's what I'll do.'

*

It wasn't long however before Dino had the opportunity to talk to Atalia. Jaq was doing some revision on local history and to help him, he and Atalia had gone up to the Devil's Tower. Being the highest point in the town meant that they could get a good view across the whole area.

Dino, having seen Jaq and Atalia set off in the direction of the tower, had quickly gathered his paper work together and headed off in the same direction. He would arrive a few minutes later to make it look coincidental.

'What a surprise!' declared Dino on arrival. 'Jaq, you really are taking your studies very seriously…and may I say how wonderful your revision is coming along. Greta told me that your sister here is helping you.'

Atalia looked surprised and then lowered her head. She didn't want her help to cause any kind of trouble.

Dino looked at Atalia. 'Do you know anything about archaeology, Atalia?'

'A little bit,' said Atalia modestly.

'Well, I have been studying this tower for a long time Atalia,' Dino continued. 'It's fascinating, you know – it's stones, it's history, it's dynasty…'

'He has…' said Jaq interrupting. 'Marco and I found him up here one evening looking at all the stones. That was the night you met Mr. Tonella, wasn't it, Dino?'

Dino's face went red. 'Yes, that's right. But let's not worry about that. I was merely trying to find out about the foundations of the tower,' he continued. 'In fact, I was wondering whether the tower had ever had a devil living in it.'

'It didn't,' replied Atalia.

'Oh, you know that, do you?' said Dino starting to get excited but trying hard to not show it.

'Everyone knows that!' said Jaq. 'I thought someone as clever as you, Dino, knew that it was only called the Devil's Tower because the people didn't know who built it so tall that they assumed it was the devil himself.'

'Yes, of course I knew that,' laughed Dino. 'Then who did build it, Atalia?'

This was the moment Dino was waiting for. Whatever Atalia said now would become a moment of a dream come true or an absolute nightmare.

'We don't know,' replied Atalia. 'But I know where the answer would be.'

'You do?' responded Dino excitedly. 'Where, Atalia, where?'

'In the foundations,' said Atalia in a matter of fact voice.

Jaq laughed as he watched the excitement on Dino's face turn to complete hopelessness. 'Bad luck, Dino. I guess you'll never know the answer to your question.'

Dino turned his back to them both. So, he thought to himself, I don't know any more than I did when I came here. I also don't know if Atalia knows anymore than she is giving away.

*

Jaq and Atalia had gone to bed by the time Greta got home but they were quickly awoken by the noise of her singing and calling as she came in the door. This was unusual as normally Greta came in quietly so as to not disturb them.

'Jaq,…Atalia,…quickly…' cried Greta's voice from downstairs.

Both of them came rushing out of their rooms and down the stairs to see what was going on. Perhaps she is drunk, thought Jaq.

Greta was stood in the middle of the living room holding a cushion and dancing around the room with it under the dim light of the table lamp in the corner.

'What is it, mother?' asked Jaq, rubbing away the sleepy dust in his eyes.

'It's true,' exclaimed Greta. 'Enzo did come all the way to San Gimignano because of me. He wants us to work together, make a bakery together and sell bread all over Tuscany.'

'Well that's brilliant,' said Atalia. 'I'm so pleased for you.'

'It's wonderful,' said Greta. 'I never believed that I could be so happy again. Sit here and let me tell you all about it.' For the next hour and a half Greta re-lived the whole evening again, word for word, action for action. It was about one thirty in the morning before Jaq politely excused himself to go to bed.

'Oh, Atalia,' said Greta, after Jaq had gone upstairs, 'there's still one thing I haven't told you or Jaq, but I think you might have guessed.'

'He's asked you to marry him,' said Atalia with a big smile on her face.

'Yes, he has…' replied Greta, beaming all over her face. 'And I said yes, Atalia, I said yes!'

The two of them hugged one another before Greta grabbed Atalia by the arm and they danced around the living room together.

'June, Atalia, June… that's the month we are going to get married. Mr. Tonella has already said we can use the hotel for the ceremony. Everyone in San

Gimignano will be invited. Life will take on a whole new beginning.'

They laughed, clapped and danced around the living room again until both of them were so tired that they decided some sleep was in need. Greta, who was completely overtired, decided she would sleep on the sofa.

Atalia said goodnight and went upstairs to bed. Lying her head on her pillow, she could see the moon shining in the night sky outside her bedroom window. How wonderful, thought Atalia, that the moon reflects the brightness of the sun and in doing so, becomes an expression of that which brings light and life into the darkness of the situation. Similarly, that's why I'm here, she thought.

'Oh well,' Atalia said to herself, 'the problem here is nearly solved. It won't be long until June – just a few weeks!'

*

Chapter 19

Dino sat up in bed. *The photo! That was the answer – the tunnels underneath the Tonella's hotel. They would reach the foundations of the Devil's Tower! If he could just reach those foundations, he would know for sure if it really was his family ancestors who had built the tower. He would need help of course, particularly on accessing the tunnels from the Tonellas hotel.* He reached over to his bedside table, turned on his mobile phone and pressed speed-dial.

*

The following weeks went by quite quickly. There was so much for everybody to be occupied with. Greta was busy with Enzo making wedding preparations. Mr. Tonella had suggested that the whole town participate in one way or another – with flowers, food, decorations and much more. Everyone in San Gimignano was invited for what was going to be a three-day celebration.

Mr. Tonella had drawn up a wedding plan that commenced with a spectacular dinner on the Friday evening, followed by an important announcement that he himself would make about an exciting new development. The Saturday would be the wedding ceremony in the morning followed by photos in the hotel's extensive grounds. The afternoon would hold the reception meal before an evening of music and dancing. The Sunday would be a grand breakfast before guests checked out. The hotel would accommodate as many guests as it could for the ceremony, considering that certain rooms had already been reserved.

Jaq was the busiest of all people. He was trying to help his mother with planning the wedding, help Mr. Tonella out at the hotel, and finish revising for his final exams. Atalia, likewise, was trying to help both Greta and Jaq as well as visiting the Tonella's hotel as much as possible. Mr. Tonella had asked Atalia to help prepare his special announcement and ensure that everything was ready. He had sworn her to secrecy although Alina also knew.

*

It was about one week before the wedding that an unusual gentleman turned up to check into the hotel. He arrived in a brand-new, black Mercedes. The paintwork gleamed in the sunlight. Out of the car stepped a tall, thin man wearing a three-piece silver-coloured suit. He was clearly very wealthy and very important. Atalia could tell by the way that he conducted himself that he was staying at the hotel on business.

'Good afternoon, signor. Welcome to the Tonella Hotel,' said Mr. Tonella very warmly. 'I am Mr. Tonella, the proprietor.'

'Buona giornata,' replied the gentlemen. 'My name is Alessandro Du Lupe.'

Strange, thought Atalia, who had been eaves-dropping into the conversation. *Another Du Lupe!* This man would need watching. She determined that she would be at the hotel as often as possible to see what this gentleman did, said or any clues that she might get as to who he actually was. There was a shadow of doubt in her mind that he was a genuine relative of Signor Du Lupe, the genuine philosopher. He bore no resemblance to him as it was.

Mr. Tonella made him welcome and Alessandro seemed to settle himself into the hotel quite quickly. It wasn't long however before Alessandro noticed that wherever he went in the hotel, there seemed to be a girl following him.

'Can I help you?' Alessandro asked Atalia on about the third day of being followed.

'Yes...you can...' replied Atalia cautiously. 'Do you know anything about philosophy?'

'Philosophy?! Why, no!' replied Alessandro. 'Whatever gave you that idea?'

'Common sense is genius dressed in it's working clothes,' responded Atalia, quoting the poet Ralph Waldo Emerson.

'I'm sorry...I'm not understanding you,' said Alessandro.

'I just thought that you might be into philosophy,' said Atalia quite dismissively. 'What are you interested in?'

'History and archaeology,' replied Alessandro. 'That's why I am here in San Gimignano. Business, you know.'

By now, Mr. Tonella was pouring Alessandro a glass of red wine. He immediately interrupted the conversation.

'History and archaeology?' he enquired. 'Who are you working for here in San Gimignano?'

'Oh, I am working independently,' replied Alessandro. 'I am researching the history of tunnels that went through Tuscany and I believe there are some here in San Gimignano.'

'What a coincidence that you are staying here,' exclaimed Mr. Tonella. 'I have something amazing to show you,' and he immediately led Alessandro over to the door in the corridor that led into the tunnels.

Coincidence? Wondered Atalia. I'm not sure. She wasn't convinced that a gentleman by the name of Du Lupe who had an interest in tunnels turning up at the hotel was particularly a coincidence.

'Keep an eye on him, Jaq,' Atalia told him. 'There's something mysterious about him.'

*

Atalia's opinion however changed over the next couple of days. She had spent time talking to Alessandro about the tunnels and he had been very knowledgeable and convincing in the way he had communicated about the rock and stone formations, the water canals and the history of the Tuscan traders. Atalia found it all very intriguing and came to put more confidence in Alessandro. She had completely put out of her mind the question about his surname, perhaps because she had been too busy.

*

It was Wednesday and the wedding was now only two days away. Everyone was still quite frantic. The hotel was nearly ready with the banqueting suite all set up with the exception of the flowers. Enzo had organised a wonderful menu for the various meals and Mr. Tonella's chef was busy ordering in all the necessary ingredients. Atalia had been busy organising the seating arrangements at dinner. She was a little surprised to find that Signor Alessandro was on the list – clearly Mr. Tonella had added his name on it for it was written in his black scribbly handwriting that was undeniably his. Even more surprising was the fact that Dino Salvucci and his family were on the list. Somehow, Atalia thought, she hadn't expected him to be there, particularly after the incident between him and Mr. Tonella. Still, if the whole village of San Gimignano was invited that would include the Salvuccis. Mr. Tonella had also gone to the trouble of organising a separate area for the children.

Atalia had also been helping Mrs. Tonella organise the hotel bedrooms. There were various guests who were going to be staying over for the two nights. This included Greta's nephews and nieces (whom Atalia had never met as they lived in the south of addition to a few other distant friends. Grᴇᴛᴀ Atalia would also have their own individuaɪ bedrooms. Although offered his own room, Jaq declined. He gave no reason as to why.

*

Jaq was, by now, quite stressed so both Greta and Atalia refrained from asking him too many questions or giving him any extra responsibilities. The exams had started and, so far, Jaq had sat his Latin paper and his Mathematics paper.

'How was the exam?' Atalia had politely enquired.

'Don't ask,' said Jaq. 'I was sure I was doing fine until I turned the page.'

'Why?'

Jaq's eyes lifted and his face scowled. 'Because that's where the exam started. The front cover was easy – you just had to write your name, date of birth and your candidate number. It was after that all the trouble started.'

Atalia smiled. 'You mean, the whole exam was hard...'

'Yes...' replied Jaq. 'There were loads of things I couldn't remember. I somehow need someone to magic all the information in my mind. Hey! You wouldn't like to disguise yourself as me and do the exams for me, would you?'

'Very funny, Jaq,' replied Atalia. 'I think that they might notice… I am both younger, smaller and more intelligent than you.'

Jaq stuck his tongue at her as Atalia left the room. He picked up his revision books and started looking at them again. *Tomorrow, Thursday, wouldn't be so bad. The exam was Italian. Surely anyone could pass an exam in their own language!* It was Friday's exams that he was the most worried about – Geography and Philosophy.

*

When Jaq arrived back home after school on Thursday, he was more relaxed. His Italian exams had gone well, and he was home by lunchtime. Greta was out having her hair done. Atalia was at the hotel putting out all the name cards on the banqueting tables and helping to put all the flowers around the room which had now arrived. Jaq therefore grabbed his revision books. This would be his last opportunity for revising and he needed to make the most of every minute.

Two hours later, the philosophy book laid strewn on the floor having been hurled across the room by a very impatient, confused and agitated Jaq. The Geography book was likewise lying on the bed in a very bedraggled state. Jaq was playing a game on his I-phone in an attempt to relieve his tension and frustration. If only he could be like Atalia, he thought to himself, then I could pass the exams easily. He imagined himself walking into the exam room the next day, opening the test paper, looking at the questions and thinking to himself 'Oh, these are so easy,' before writing the answers down in half the time that everybody else could. He would then come home and relax. Then, on Sunday evening, before the next week's exams, he would…

His mind stopped. 'Hang on a minute,' he said out loud to himself. 'There is a way I can pass my exams easily!' He was glad that no-one was there to hear him, but the thought that had entered his mind was an ingenious idea.

*

Friday morning came. Jaq sat at the breakfast table as cool as a cucumber, munching the continental breakfast his mother had made for him.

'What exams are you doing today, Jaq?' asked Greta.

'Oh…nothing too hard…philosophy and geography…' replied Jaq casually.

'You seem very calm about the whole thing,' noted Greta, watching her son slouching in his chair, chewing on some buttered croissant and cheese.

'Of course, I am,' replied Jaq. 'I've been well-taught, haven't I? Atalia has done a good job at making sure I know all that I need to.' He smiled at Atalia.

'That's kind of you to say so, Jaq. I hope it all goes well,' she replied.

With that, Jaq finished his breakfast, rushed upstairs to clean his teeth, fetched his school bag and then headed off to school. He was feeling quietly confident.

*

Atalia spent the rest of the day helping Greta pack her things. This was not an easy task as Greta insisted on taking nearly everything in the event of any unforeseen circumstances. She even packed a hamper of food in case for any reason she either felt hungry or the caterers hadn't prepared enough. Atalia tried to assure her that everything would be fine, but Greta's reply was 'better safe than sorry'. Greta then phoned to book a taxi for 3pm. Normally it would take no more than ten minutes to walk to the hotel, but with the multitude of cases, bags and boxes, a taxi would be needed to get everything there. Until now, everything had been going well.

It was 2pm when Atalia concluded that Greta now had everything packed and she would pack her own case. For the meantime, she would stay in her jeans, t-shirt and trainers. Later on, at the hotel, she would change into her little blue dress – the same one, she thought, I was wearing when I arrived. It still looked absolutely pristine and new. In the suitcase it went along with hair accessories, wash kit, changes of clothes for the next couple of days, her present for Greta and Enzo which she had made from some fabric given to her by Georgia in the dress shop, and some other accessories.

It was only as she was putting the last few things in the suitcase that Atalia found herself panicking.

'Greta, have you seen my bag?'

'What bag, Atalia?'

'Oh, you know, the one I normally carry around with me.'

'The one that I never know what's inside,' replied Greta.

'Yes, that one,' said Atalia.

'No, I haven't…'

Atalia hunted all over. The bag can't have gone missing, she thought. She ran down the stairs to look into the living room, the kitchen, even outside in the garden, but the bag was not there.

'Whatever is the matter?' said Greta coming into the bedroom. She had never seen Atalia in such a state.

'My bag is gone,' exclaimed Atalia. 'Without it, I can't…' She didn't want to finish her sentence. She sat on the bed and thought whilst Greta put her arm around her.

'Atalia, whatever is in your bag I am sure is not necessary for today. We are going to the hotel to enjoy my wedding celebration. As you said to me, everything is sorted. Now stop worrying.' She smiled at Atalia.

It was at this moment that Atalia wanted to tell her the truth about the sticks and the stones and how much of a difference those items made – *how without them she would never have known about the time when Greta fell off the balcony in advance of the accident. She looked at Greta standing at her bedroom door. How can I ruin her pre-wedding night?* She thought. *I must go ahead without my bag. After all, Greta is right. Nothing is going to go wrong.*

She got up from her bed, smiled at Greta. 'Let's go,' she said. 'You're right – I am worrying too much!'

'Perhaps Jaq will know where your bag is,' suggested Greta as they got into the taxi.

Atalia stopped in her thoughts. 'Jaq!...yes, he knows where my bag is!'

*

Chapter 20

Jaq had indeed borrowed Atalia's bag but without her permission. He figured that somehow there was a significance to the bag and that if anything could help him pass his exams then the bag could. He didn't take out the two sticks or the twelve stones, but simply laid the bag on his lap whilst taking the exams. He certainly didn't want an invigilator to see it and confiscate it. If it subsequently got lost, Atalia would never forgive him.

If he was totally truthful with himself, he knew that he shouldn't have just taken it. He should have asked Atalia and found out in advance whether it would help him with the questions. Only now did the thought cross his mind that perhaps the sticks and stones did need to be laid out in the order that he had seen Atalia do the night he had filmed her in the garden. It wasn't really possible though. He would have to hope that the bag would just bring good luck. He held it tight in his hand whilst the invigilator started to brief the candidates. Then came the starting moment:

'You have three hours. The exam starts now...'

Jaq opened the philosophy paper and stared at the questions. There was a question on Aristotle, another on Plato, another on Socrates and another on the ontological argument. Jaq had studied all these in class before. He had revised them with Atalia who had given him some little tips for remembering who had said what. But at this moment, Jaq realised something…he was stuck, and this next three hours were going to feel really long.

'Oh, please help,' whispered Jaq to the bag on his lap. 'Give me something to get started…'

The bag however didn't reply. It sat there lifeless. Jaq even gave the bag a little shake to see if somehow some kind of inspiration would come to him, but it didn't. He sighed a great sigh. Taking Atalia's bag had been a completely waste of time. He felt more incompetent than usual, particularly as he hadn't bothered to revise hard. *How could he have left himself believe that a simple bag belonging to his sister was going to make him a genius? Clearly it was Atalia who was naturally intelligent, not anything to do with her little ritual in the garden every morning and evening.* He felt such an idiot.

The three hours dragged by. He tried his best to answer as many questions as possible but with limited success. His mind was more on what Atalia's reaction would have been when she realised that the bag was gone. He thought about how she and Greta would be getting everything packed for the hotel. *Perhaps, he told himself, he should have stayed at the hotel himself after all.* What he did or didn't do didn't see so important anymore.

He looked over at Marco who was scribbling answers down on his paper as quickly as possible whilst rubbing his hand across his forehead on a number of occasions. Further down the hall was Martina who was conscientiously writing away. She was bound to pass the exam. There wasn't much that she didn't know now-a-days.

Eventually the exam came to an end and Jaq felt relieved to be back out in the fresh air again. There would be a one-hour break before the Geography exam. He looked at Atalia's bag one more time before burying it in the bottom of his rucksack, determined to return it to Atalia as soon as possible and try and come out with a plausible explanation for having taken it.

*

The taxi driver safely deposited Greta and Atalia at the Tonella's hotel. It was the first time that Greta had seen the hotel since it had been decorated. There were some beautiful white lilies in the reception area and a special welcome sign for all the guests with a reminder of the schedule for the wedding event. Many of Greta's guests would be arriving between 6pm and 7pm, giving her plenty of time to unpack, get changed and be ready to welcome them.

Enzo was no-where to be seen. He had, apparently, informed Mrs. Tonella at reception that he wouldn't make an appearance until just before the dinner started. He wanted Greta to be the centre of attention with no infringement on his part, so he had taken himself off to Lucca, another town in Tuscany, for the afternoon.

It was shortly after Greta's arrival that Atalia introduced her to Alessandro.

'Signor Alessandro, it is a pleasure to meet you. Atalia has been telling me about your wonderful interest in the history and archaeology of this town.'

'Signora, yes… I have been honoured to learn much in this last week from the discoveries made by both Mr. Tonella and your daughter Atalia. Both have been very obliging to my research.'

He smiled at Atalia. 'I think Mr. Tonella has a surprise for everyone later tonight, don't you think?'

'He certainly does,' replied Atalia. 'I am sure the town will be most excited.'

*

By 6pm the guests had all arrived except Jaq. Alina had received a text asking if she could apologise to Greta and Atalia that he would be late. Jaq could have text his mother himself but didn't want to end up in a difficult conversation. Greta tried to phone Jaq back when she received the message, but Jaq had turned his phone off.

Everyone was in the dining room, sat around chatting and laughing with one another. Enzo had arrived back from Lucca and was sitting next to Greta on the top table, holding hands, smiling, laughing and hugging her. Other relatives were sat around and Greta was introducing them one by one to Enzo who replied what an honour it was to meet them. His French accent didn't seem to surprise anyone particularly and all agreed with Greta that Enzo was a particularly warm, kind and welcoming man.

When Jaq did arrive, he looked smart in his new suit and he quietly came over and sat next to Alina.

'Psssst,' Atalia hissed across the table. 'Have you got my bag?'

'It's at home. I left it in your bedroom,' answered Jaq, thinking that he was being helpful.

'Psssst… why did you take it?'

'Not now, Atalia. It's mum's special occasion, remember?'

Atalia felt frustrated. It had been difficult being without it all day. It left her feeling uneasy, unsure and unknowing of what future events had in store.

*

The meal itself was delicious. Mr. Tonella's chef, along with some guidance from Enzo's experience of French baking, had produced a wonderful banquet. For appetisers, they had Italian mini meatballs that were handmade and simmered in a beautiful tomato sauce. This was then followed by a spinach and mushroom salad. The main course was seabass in a white wine sauce served with carrots, mushrooms, red pepper and tomatoes. The second mains was seared parmesan risotto cakes with a beautiful seafood sauce. Next came sorbet, lemon flavour mixed with a little alcohol to cleanse the palate in time for dessert, which was tiramisu. Finally, it was time for cake decorated with sugar almonds.

Everyone was so full as well as enjoying glasses of Prosecco, red wine, rose wine, white wine and much more.

It was only when everyone was completely satisfied that Mr. Tonella requested that the music be turned down and that a microphone be brought to him.

'Ladies and gentlemen,' he started. 'We hope you have had a most enjoyable dinner this evening in honour of our wonderful friend, Greta Alfonsi, and her betrothed, Signor Enzo.'

Everyone in the room clapped and applauded. Greta turned a mild shade of red with embarrassment whilst Enzo stood, raised a glass and smiled before promptly sitting down again.

'But,...' Mr. Tonella continued. 'Tonight, is also a special night for the Tonella Hotel and for the Tonella family.' He cleared his throat. 'As many of you know, we discovered, after purchasing the hotel, that there were underground tunnels. Much work has gone into exploring these tunnels and finding out where they lead. Not only that, but electric lights have been fitted inside some of the tunnels so that other people can come and walk in them safely and witness the amazing work of our ancestors who built and developed them all those many years ago. We have now completed our work and have secured a touristic route all the way from this hotel to the very centre of San Gimignano. This route will only be available to our hotel guests if they should wish to explore it; but tonight, ladies and gentlemen, the Tonella's want to share with you the honour and the privilege of visiting the tunnels. They will forever be known as the Tonella Tunnels.'

At this point, Mr. Tonella turned on the white-screen projector and showed everyone in the room photographs of the tunnels and the completed work. Everyone in the room clapped and cheered.

The tour would take place at 9:45pm and would last about half an hour, fifteen minutes each way. Mr. Tonella invited his daughter Alina, and Atalia, to lead the way. Signor Alessandro was close behind whilst Mr. Tonella accompanied the rear, ensuring that no-one got left behind.

*

When everyone returned there was a hub of chatter and excitement about all that they had seen. The route had been so clearly marked with lighting, ropes on the sides to help people down the parts with steps, and coloured arrows pointing in the right direction. The Tonella Tunnels were a success and the town people were buzzing over the new attraction that would bring much excitement to the guests who would come to see them. Mr. Tonella was already preparing great hotel breaks and packages for those who would come from neighbouring countries such as France, Germany, Croatia and further.

Eventually everyone was back in the function room having drinks and laughing. The children had been sent to bed and were probably fast asleep.

Atalia herself felt tired and was ready for an early night. The adults were all chatting amongst themselves and she could see that her absence would be noticed. She went and whispered goodnight to Greta before slipping out of the banqueting hall.

She started walking along the hotel corridor when suddenly she felt a hand on her shoulder. She turned around to see who it was.

'Good evening, Atalia, how are you?'

'I'm fine, Dino, thank you – just a bit tired.' She paused. 'What are you doing out here? Shouldn't you be in with all the guests?'

'No, I've been waiting for you. I need your help.'

'Why? What is it?'

'I need to go back into the tunnels again. I dropped something and I need to get it back.'

'What did you lose?' said Atalia, concerned.

'My wallet,' replied Dino. 'It has all my personal information in it, and I wouldn't want anyone else to pick it up.'

'I understand…' said Atalia reluctantly. 'Can't it wait until the morning, Dino?'

Dino's face turned angry and indignant. 'No…I need to get it now.'

'Okay, okay…calm down…' said Atalia, rather shocked at his response. 'I suppose it won't take long. Come on.'

Dino's voice turned calm again. 'Thank you Atalia. I'm sorry if I am causing you any inconvenience.'

Atalia led Dino to the entrance door. She opened it and stepped in with Dino following behind her. Little did either Atalia or Dino realise, but another person followed shortly behind them too.

*

They walked for about ten minutes until they came to the chamber where the water canal was. Dino was shining his torch around the room, desperately hunting for his wallet. Atalia likewise was looking along the walkway.

Eventually, Dino's voice cried out in a delighted tone. 'Atalia, I've found it…'

Atalia looked. Dino's torch was pointing to a wallet that lay a few metres behind a metal gate – nowhere near the original trail that they had gone on.

'Had did it get there?' asked Atalia, completely puzzled by the wallet's position.

'I don't know,' said Dino. 'But I need to get it back.'

'But how will we get through the gate?' asked Atalia.

Dino pushed on the gate. It squeaked as it swung back on the old hinges, revealing a pitch-black single file passageway behind it.

'Atalia, if I shine the torch, will you get it for me?'

Atalia slid past the gate and bent down to pick up the wallet off the floor. She was about to turn around when she discovered that Dino was stood right behind her.

'Well done, Atalia,' came his gruff voice. 'Now let's just keep walking and see where this passage leads, eh?'

*

Chapter 21

They carried on walking for another five minutes or so. The passageways were dark, and it was only the light shining from Dino's torch that prevented them from crashing or hurting themselves. Atalia didn't know these particular passageways and was concerned to where they would lead.

All the time, a million questions were going through her mind. *Why was Dino wanting to explore these passageways? What was he hoping to achieve? How was she going to get out of this situation?* She blamed herself for having not looked after her bag more carefully. *If she had had her sticks and stones, then she would have been able to foresee what was going to happen and avoided this precarious situation.* Now she was unsure where she was or where they were going. She didn't exactly trust the company she was with either.

They eventually entered a large chamber, similar to the one that had passed through earlier, only this one was clearly at a deeper level and completely in darkness. Dino shone his torch around. 'Ah ha,' he said, pointing at a corner of the chamber which had some kind of inscription written upon it. 'What does this say, Atalia?'

Atalia went over and looked at it. 'I don't know,' she replied.

'Come on…' said Dino impatiently. 'You must know. You know everything!'

Atalia looked hard again. She could see that the writing was very similar to the other inscriptions she had seen, but there was no way of knowing what it said. An idea came to her mind however – perhaps she could bluff it.

'Ooozto…ghermanji….uzzeeehemphadinga…' she started to read, knowing too well that she was making up each and every word as she ran her finger along the inscription.

'What does it mean?' cried an exasperated Dino.

'Difficult to translate,' said Atalia, biding her time, knowing that she would need to make the interpretation as believable as possible. She thought hard about what Dino might be interested in. *Maybe treasure? Maybe gold? Or something to do with the Devil's Tower? Or about the Ardinghellis considering he was related to one?*

She decided to combine the ideas together. She took a deep breath and prepared to deliver her most convincing speech yet.

'Ooozto means treasure,' she started. 'Ghermanji was another name for the Ardinghellis, although I doubt you've heard of them,' she bluffed.

'Go on, go on,' said Dino, his voice becoming quite excitable.

Gullible, thought Atalia, completely gullible…

'Uzzeeehemphadinga…' she continued 'means near the Devil's Tower.'

All was silent. She turned around but could see nothing because of the pitch-black darkness. Even Dino's torch bulb was so faint she could hardly see it.

'Dino?'

'Great, Atalia… well done. You have done well.'

'Why?' asked Atalia, curious to know what this expedition had all been about.

'Because at last, I can make the Ardinghelli name great again! Finally, I know that the Salvucci family did not build the Devil's Tower for you have just proved that the Ardinghelli family hid their treasure under the tower. By following this route further, I shall find the treasure.'

Dino sat down on the floor. 'By the time I have found it, Atalia – thanks to your help – I shall make history. My family ancestry will be acknowledged as the greatest in San Gimignano and the Salvucci family's name will be purely insignificant. That, Atalia,' he continued, 'is why I came back to San Gimignano. I have believed for many years that my ancestors established this town and were the greatest people that ever lived here. It was only when the Salvucci family also were around that they tried to take the credit for themselves. But no more… now I shall prove that the Ardinghellis were the greatest.'

Atalia gulped. *What have I done?* She thought to herself. *I have just made up a whole lot of nonsense and deceived a man into thinking that he is Italy's next greatest legend.*

'Not only that…' continued Dino, 'but once I have that treasure, I shall make a compulsory purchase of the Tonella's hotel and rename it 'The Ardinghelli'. The history of Mr. Tonella and his Salvucci heritage will be wiped out from the minds of the people of San Gimignano.' He paused. 'Tonella Tunnels indeed,' he continued, 'no way. It shall never be. I shall meet with Mr. Tonella immediately in the morning and tell him of the discovery.'

There was the sound of footsteps approaching the chamber and a dim light of another torch. As the person drew closer, Dino recognised the voice of the person calling. He got up off the floor and headed to the darkest corner of the chamber.

'It's Mr. Tonella,' muttered Dino. 'Quick, Atalia, come here. Now don't say anything – let me do the talking!'

Mr. Tonella entered the chamber and shone his torch around. The dim light reaching closer and closer to where Dino and Atalia were, before shining in a different direction. They hadn't been seen.

'They can't have gone much further now,' said Mr. Tonella to himself. 'This passage doesn't continue for much further. When I see that Dino, I shall…'

'Do what?!' cried out Dino provocatively.

'Where are you?' shouted Mr. Tonella. 'I want to talk to you. You have violated my invitation to the hotel and completely ruined a very delightful evening. Now get out of my tunnels or you'll be sorry when I get my hands on you!'

'Calm down Salvucci!' yelled Dino back aggressively. 'Before you start getting hostile, remember I have Atalia here. I think you might need to listen to what she has to say.'

Atalia stepped forward to go towards Mr. Tonella, but Dino grabbed her and pulled her back. 'No, you don't,' he said. 'You're the only evidence I've got - you're staying right here.'

No, I'm not, thought Atalia. She took a deep breath, lifted her left knee, swung her foot forward ready to bring it back hard on Dino's shin, but it proved unsuccessful for Dino predicted the move and stopped her from kicking him.

Mr. Tonella's torch swung around the chamber again, looking for both Dino and Atalia. The light caught a little of Atalia's blue dress. 'Atalia, just say whatever it is that Dino wants you to say and then we can all get out of here.'

'That's not easy...' replied Atalia, trying to wriggle herself loose from Dino. She knew that this situation had a lose-lose outcome. Her mind wrestled with what to do. *If she told Mr. Tonella the same lie that she had told*

Dino, then the whole deception could cause huge troubles for the Tonella family – aside from which, she herself could get into trouble for lying. But would anyone know? she thought to herself. *On the other hand, if she said that she had made it up, then goodness knows what Dino would do next?*

'Come on, Atalia, tell Mr. Tonella about the writing on the wall. Tell him what you told me about how these tunnels don't actually belong to him!' screamed Dino, still holding Atalia tightly.

'What?!' screamed Mr. Tonella. 'Is this true, Atalia?'

'I don't want to say anything,' replied Atalia.

'Alright…I'll tell you,' started Dino. 'Atalia led me down to these chambers and showed me an inscription on the wall. It read…' He paused, trying to remember the words that Atalia had said. 'I can't remember the exact words, but they speak of the treasure of my family ancestry, the Ardinghellis, being buried in these tunnels near the Devil's Tower.' He paused again. 'These tunnels don't belong to you, Mr. Tonella, nor your family ancestry of the Salvucci family – they belong to me – the rightful heir of the Ardinghelli family. Tell him, Atalia – tell him!'

'I told you I'm not going to say anything,' reiterated Atalia. 'I'm not getting involved.'

*

Dino let go of Atalia. The arguing between Dino and Mr. Tonella continued for what felt like ages with both men pushing and shoving each other. It was only when another set of footsteps arrived in the dark chamber that both men stopped, realising that neither of them were getting anywhere.

A bright light shone around the chamber from the lamp light of its latest arrival. It was Alessandro. Atalia was relieved to see him. She knew now that no matter what happened between Dino and Mr. Tonella, she would get out of the tunnels safely.

'What's happening here, brother?' asked Alessandro, looking directly at Dino. 'I knew that you were up to something when I received your phone call.'

Mr. Tonella flung his arms up into the air in great frustration. 'Well, that's great, that is!' he shouted aggressively. 'You're a real surprise, Alessandro. I thought you were genuinely interested in the tunnels here at San Gimignano. Now I find out that you are brother to this troublemaker here. Trying to drive me out, aren't you? Well, you won't get away with this. It might be two against one, but I'll take you both on!' He threw his jacket on the floor and started rolling up his shirt sleeves ready for a fight.

'Wait a minute!' said Alessandro. 'Let me explain before this goes horribly wrong.'

Mr. Tonella put his fists on his hips and waited for what he anticipated was going to be the lamest explanation he had ever heard in his life.

Alessandro took a deep breath. 'Yes, Dino is my brother. He called me about ten days ago to say that there were some underground tunnels that I would be interested in at your hotel. I immediately drove over to San Gimignano and checked in with you nearly a week ago. Since then, you know that I have been exploring the tunnels and reporting to you about what I have discovered.' He paused. 'It is my profession, Mr. Tonella. I did show you my qualifications. Atalia will also tell you that everything I have done in these tunnels has been carried out decently and properly.'

Atalia nodded.

'What I don't know,' Alessandro continued, 'is why these tunnels mattered to Dino so much although I think I might have a good guess. When I saw Dino and Atalia entering the tunnels after dinner this evening, I knew that something was happening. That's why I let you know, Mr. Tonella. I would have come with you, but I received a call on my mobile which couldn't wait, but it looks like I have arrived at just the right time.'

'I am trying to explain to Mr. Tonella here that these tunnels don't belong to him,' said Dino turning on his brother.

'Oh, but they do,' replied Alessandro. 'He owns the hotel.'

'Not for much longer,' replied Dino. 'Atalia and I have proof that these tunnels belonged to our family heritage, Alessandro. The tunnels were built by our ancestors, the Ardinghellis. Not only that, but there is Ardinghelli treasure hidden down here somewhere and when I find it, I shall purchase the hotel from this Salvucci here and our family name will be great again.'

Alessandro sighed and sat down. 'Is that what this is all about, brother?'

Dino came and stood next to Alessandro. 'What do you mean, is that all this is about?' he mimicked.

'Atalia, show me the writing,' said Alessandro.

Atalia moved reluctantly over to the writing she had interpreted for Dino and pointed at it. She was about to be exposed for lying.

'This does say 'Ardinghelli'', said Alessandro pointing at the first of the words.

'See? I told you!' said Dino, pointing at the writing.

'But Atalia misunderstood the other two words here,' said Alessandro, continuing to point at the words. 'You see, Atalia, do you see the little line you missed? That little line changes the whole meaning.'

Atalia looked at Alessandro. He was smiling and she began to realise that he wasn't going to give her away.

'This word here says 'Salvucci'', continued Alessandro, pointing at the second word.

'Ha!' cried Mr. Tonella, 'that puts an end to your claim, Dino.'

'What about the third word?' cried Dino in desperation.

'The third word means...' He paused as if some dramatic music was about to play like the moment before a contestant finds out the answer to a quiz question. 'The third word means...'forever!''

He looked at Dino and Mr. Tonella, who both stood there speechless. Atalia looked at Alessandro, then at the two men, and then chuckled to herself.

'It's not funny,' cried Dino, seeing Atalia laughing.

'Oh, but it is,' said Alessandro. 'I can explain, but not in this light. I have all the paperwork back in my room. The phone call I took moments before coming down here also confirmed my suspicions. Come on, let me show you. Come on, Atalia – you will find this fascinating as well.'

Mr. Tonella and Dino just continued staring at each other. *The Salvuccis and the Ardinghellis together, surely not.*

*

The three men and Atalia were sat in the hotel bar until very early into the morning. Alessandro brought out of his briefcase a map he had made of all the tunnels in San Gimignano and the surrounding areas. All four of them studied the routes intensely and found it fascinating that their ancestors had achieved some great projects.

'The history behind the chamber that we were in tonight goes back to a story that hardly anyone knows, not even in San Gimignano. One of the Ardinghellis fell hopelessly in love with the daughter of a Salvucci,' continued Alessandro. 'Because the two families were great rivals, the only time they could ever meet was whilst they were in the tunnels. He worked on the underground canals whilst she was the daughter of a baker, so she used to bring down food for him. They met in that large, dark chamber for fear of being discovered. It was only after they became engaged that he carved those words into the chamber walls – a sign that the Ardinghellis and Salvuccis would one day come together in peace and harmony.'

He took a sip of his drink.

'What about the treasure?' asked Mr. Tonella, suddenly concerned that Dino may still have some claim on the tunnels.

'It never existed. It was a myth that treasure lay under the ruins of the Devil's Tower. We will never know for sure who built the tower, but the treasure was a figment of someone's imagination all those years ago.'

Alessandro looked at both men. 'You haven't been taking things that seriously, have you?'

Dino hung his head low. 'I'm afraid I have. I came back to San Gimignano to restore our family name, Alessandro. I have been teaching history and philosophy and using it as an excuse to study the area around the Devil's Tower. Then when I learnt about the Tonella Tunnels, I just knew that this was the opportunity. Having met Atalia, I discovered that she would be the only person to lead me to the treasure. Oh! I feel such an idiot!' He put his hands into his head. 'I'm sorry, Atalia. I'm sorry, Mr. Tonella.'

Mr. Tonella looked at Dino with compassion. Then he suddenly laughed out loud.

'Do you like teaching, Dino?'

Dino looked at him strangely. 'Why?'

'I have an idea,' continued Mr. Tonella. 'We cannot change the name of the tunnels as everyone here in San Gimignano knows them as the Tonella Tunnels. But...' he paused. 'Why don't you take all the information from your brother here and come and work for me?'

'Doing what?!' asked Dino rather intimidated at the suggestion.

'Tour guide,' replied Mr. Tonella. 'Look together, we could make this the greatest legend of Italy. Forget Romeo and Juliet...think, Ardinghellis and Salvuccis forever!'

Dino looked at Mr. Tonella as the idea went through his mind, both with disbelief and curiosity. Mr. Tonella kept his eyes fixed on Dino. Atalia and Alessandro didn't know who was going to make the next move.

'Deal,' said Dino. 'I will hand my notice in at the start of the summer and start straightaway. Together, we will make San Gimignano famous again!'

*

Chapter 22

The rest of the wedding ceremony was delightful. Greta and Enzo became the talk of the town for many weeks and months to come after. Plans to open a brand-new bakery and patisserie were put in place as a combination of French and Italian bread and pastries were introduced to the people of San Gimignano.

Many more people were also coming around to dinner in the evenings, some invited, others uninvited but simply seemed to appear at the house about the same time as a meal was being served. Greta was initially quite suspicious, but very quickly learnt that the local people were intrigued by the sort of food that Enzo and Greta were creating together. Even Mr. Tonella's chef dropped in every so often to gain some new ideas from Enzo for evening meals at the hotel.

'It's not a problem,' said Enzo in his modest French accent. 'It just means a little of France has now infiltrated Italian culture.'

Enzo also had many friends who came to visit him in Italy simply to taste some genuine Italian dishes.

*

Alessandro had left the Tonella's hotel a short time after the wedding, delighted to see that his brother Dino had got over his hostility towards Mr. Tonella and that the two of them would now be working together. He gave both Dino and Mr. Tonella a copy of his paperwork and encouraged them to make a good success of his endeavour with the tunnels in San Gimignano.

'I am happy to recommend this hotel's tunnels to the tourism and archaeological board,' he said. 'They would be most interested and as a result you could have many more people coming into San Gimignano.

'Thank you,' said Mr. Tonella. 'Your help here has been greatly appreciated. We hope you will come back again.'

'Of course,' replied Alessandro, slightly surprised that this hadn't been an obvious conclusion. 'I will want to see how successful you have become.'

*

Atalia came to the hotel to see Alessandro depart.

'It was a joy to meet you, Atalia,' said Alessandro, shaking her hand. 'I'm most grateful for your help.'

'What did I do?' asked Atalia, quite surprised.

'You pointed out those words which has made such a difference to life here in San Gimignano. My brother should not have been so deceitful and prejudice; but by you pointing out those words, the Ardinghelli dynasty and the Salvucci dynasty can work together again.'

'Alessandro...' began Atalia, almost nervous to ask. 'Those words...do they mean what you said they mean? Did those little lines really make that much of a difference?'

'I think you know the answer to that,' replied Alessandro with an even bigger smile and a twinkle in his eye. He bent down to whisper in her ear. 'Whether they do or whether they don't, no-one but you and I are ever going to know any different, are they?'

*

Jaq had apologised to Atalia for taking her bag on the day. 'I just wanted to do well in my Geography and Philosophy exams,' he explained to Atalia. 'I just knew that somehow there was something about that bag that is significant to you and I thought…well…' his voice trailed off, almost to a silence.

'Look, Jaq,' replied Atalia. 'My bag cannot give you success. The sticks and stones don't work like that.'

'Well, what do they do?'

'They are a reminder of something far bigger than just doing well, Jaq. Firstly, the twelve stones and the two sticks have to be correctly placed, but they are still powerless – they are just sticks and stones.'

'But I don't get it…' continued Jaq. 'How is it that you are able to understand things that are going to happen when you have them, but you can't without them?'

'It's what they represent,' replied Atalia. 'The stones speak of order and the sticks speak of humility. That is why every morning and every night I spend time reflecting on these things. Everything has an order, Jaq, and if we keep everything in order, then all will go well. In staying humble and realising that there is more to life than just ourselves, we can be better agents of change to those around us.'

'Is that what you do then?' asked Jaq. His face had a look of curiosity and it was as if a piece of the puzzle was beginning to come together. 'Are you an agent of change?'

Atalia smiled. 'What changes do you see, Jaq?'

Jaq started thinking hard. A lot of things had certainly changed. He remembered what he had been like when Atalia had first arrived in their lives. He thought about Dino and Mr. Tonella and how two rival ancestries were now working together. He thought about how his mother Greta was no longer the person she had been.

'But...' Jaq started, but Atalia had walked out of the room. His mind continued to ponder over everything and everyone he knew – *Marco, Alina, Martina, Enzo,.. yes, people and situations had definitely changed.*

*

When Jaq's results arrived, he was reluctant to open them. *On one hand*, he told himself, *it wouldn't matter - he was going to be working for Mr. Tonella and learning how to be successful in the hotel industry. On the other hand, he thought, it would be good to have done well.*

Alina was stood at his side when he opened them. She herself had gained some excellent results, and now she wanted to be there to give Jaq some encouragement.

'Well, come on, Jaq,' said Greta excitedly. 'Let's see what you have achieved.'

He pulled the paper out and looked at it carefully. His expression looked quite surprised, then one eyebrow raised with suspicion, before he then chuckled to himself.

'What's so funny?' said Alina.

'Well…' said Jaq. 'I passed all my subjects apart from two.'

'Congratulations!' exclaimed Greta, throwing down the tea-towel that she had in her hands and hugging Jaq as hard as she could. Alina also joined the hug and the three of them jumped up and down together for joy.

'I knew you could do it,' said Greta.

'Well, I did have a lot of help,' said Jaq, 'and I appreciate it.'

He looked at Atalia who had just walked into the room. 'I need to thank you particularly,' said Jaq, giving Atalia a hug as well. 'I can't say that I have done as well as you would have done, but I am grateful. By the way, Atalia,' he continued, holding out the results paper to her. 'Have a look at the two subjects I didn't pass.'

Atalia looked at the paper. 'Geography and Philosophy,' she replied with a smirk on her face before she also chuckled.

'What is so funny about your results in those two subjects?' asked Alina, knowing that both Jaq and Atalia knew something that she didn't.

'Oh…that's between Atalia and I,' answered Jaq. 'Fools rush in, eh, Atalia?'

'Where angels fear to tread,' responded Atalia.

*

The summer holidays were busy. The weather was hot, and many tourists were visiting San Gimignano, visiting the towers, exploring the old town, buying ice-cream and taking photos of the wonderful landscape of Tuscany.

Greta and Enzo were working rigorously to produce excellent food for both the townsfolk and the tourists. Jaq was sleeping in the mornings and then behind the bar at the Tonella's hotel afternoons and evenings that Atalia hardly saw him. Even when he did have some time off, Jaq would be seen wandering out with Alina, hand in hand, enjoying one another's company.

Atalia herself had spent time in the home, tidying, cleaning and keeping herself busy. She was determined that when everyone came home, there would be some order in the house and a calming atmosphere.

*

On the 31st August, about midday, Atalia went out into the garden and sat down on the ground with her bag of stones and sticks. Being an enclosed garden, she knew that she would be undisturbed, despite hearing the noise of all the hustle and bustle going on in the street outside the front door.

She laid the stones and sticks out as she had done every morning and night, but for the first time, next to every stone, she placed a photo of the people she had come to know here in San Gimignano, including Greta, Jaq, Enzo, Alina, Mr and Mrs. Tonella, Dino and his family, and a few more. She started uttering words out of her mouth and as she did so, it was as if the stones illuminated, for they appeared to be brighter and shinier than ever before. Perhaps it was because they were now in the direct sunlight of a hot summer's day.

Atalia looked up at the sky and nodded her head with an inward knowing that her life was about to change too. The time had come for her to move on from San Gimignano. She went inside and packed her few things into a small bag, leaving everything that anyone had given her in the small bedroom that she had come to know as her own.

She wore the same blue dress that she had arrived in and took with her nothing more than she had had that day. On the kitchen table, she left a note for Greta.

There was a knock on the front door. Atalia went to open it. Carlotta was stood outside. Atalia invited her in.

'You're leaving today, aren't you, Atalia?' she said with a knowing look on her face.

'Yes…I am,' replied Atalia. 'But please don't tell anyone, Carlotta.'

'It's not my job to,' answered Carlotta. 'I knew the day that I brought you to this home that you were to live here for a purpose, and this morning, when I woke up, something inside told me that you were about to go, and I just wanted to say farewell. You have made a big difference to our lives here in San Gimignano.'

'Thank you,' said Atalia gratefully.

*

It was 6pm when Enzo and Greta got home. Enzo went and sat down in the living room, opening up the newspaper to read the daily news that he had already heard discussed so many times on the street that day. Greta was in the kitchen, preparing the evening meal. She saw the note on the table and opened it. The message was short. It read:

Dear Greta, thank you for everything. I will not forget you. The old has gone and the new has been established. My time in San Gimignano is done. Atalia.'

Greta paused, tears appearing in her eyes, as she read the little note over and over again, before folding it and putting it inside her purse beside a little photo of Atalia that she had also placed there.

*

Atalia had walked down the main street, past the Tonella's hotel and out onto the country road that led towards Siena. No-one saw her leave as everyone was so busy dealing with the hundreds of tourists that had come to San Gimignano that day.

'Goodbye, San Gimignano,' she said out loud. 'I shall never be back, but I know that what I have done will live on in the hearts of the people for a long time yet.' She turned around and started walking along the country lane. There was a sudden flash of light and Atalia was gone.

Conclusion – questions to the author

Why did you choose to set the story in San Gimignano?

I had visited San Gimignano in 2014. The whole area of Tuscany is beautiful, but the town intrigued me, particularly the towers.

Is the story historically true?

No, it's not. There are some facts in the story which are based on history – such as the fact that there were two rival families called the Salvuccis and the Ardinghellis who built a lot of the towers. The actual characters and plot line however are completely fictitious.

Did you have to do a lot of research for this book?

To a certain extent, yes. Some of the research was completed in advance. Other parts had to be researched as the book was being written.

How long has it taken you to write the book?

The ideas have been in my mind since I came back from Tuscany, but the writing of it has taken about nine months with periods of stopping and starting in between.

Is Atalia a real person?

During my time in Italy, I met someone who became the inspiration for Atalia. Her name however was not Atalia and she was just a normal person.

Did you know what the whole story was going to be before you started writing?

Most definitely not. Stories evolve as you write, and it is fascinating to see where characters and situations end up.

Will there be a sequel to this story?

Possibly... watch this space...

Did you base any of the characters on yourself or anyone you knew?

Certainly not myself. There may have been people I observed during my time in Italy in the story, but no specific people (apart from Atalia as mentioned earlier).

Where did the names come from? Did you make them up?

A lot of the time the names were made up. Looking up Italian names on Google was one of the little cheats I used.